THE

IMMORTAL

EXPLORER

KYREA'S QUEST FOR KNOWLEDGE

Book 1

KATHLEEN J. SHIELDS

THE IMMORTAL EXPLORER
Kyrea's Quest For Knowledge
Book 1

ISBN: 978-1-956581-74-4   Paperback

ISBN: 978-1-956581-67-6   Hardback

Library of Congress Control Number: 2025917555

© Copyright 2025 Cover Illustrations by Sumayya Monsoor

Canyon Lake, Texas
www.ErinGoBraghPublishing.com

TABLE OF CONTENTS

Medieval

Meanderings

"GET THAT GIRL!" The armored knight declared from atop his steadfast stead. His voice echoed as he spurred his horse down the dusty path, leading a battalion of knights in hot pursuit. Though the girl was fleeing with remarkable speed, the knights' fears were only heightened by the sight of her riding an unfamiliar two-wheeled contraption. It moved with such swiftness and grace that they were convinced she must be a witch! Anyone who was able to outpace them without the aid of a horse MUST be a witch!

Watching from afar was a dragon; a dragon who had met the most curious young girl that morning. As he thought back to the events of the morning, he couldn't help but chuckle.

Having been completely camouflaged within the green terrain, still as stone, and certain no mere

2

mortal could have ever laid eyes on him, she just wandered up to him, placed her palm on his nose and said *hi, my name's Kyrea.* Refusing to move, even to part an eyelid for a quick peek, he remained still as she kept talking. Though he could have made her into a meal, he was intrigued by her bright young voice. His desire to take a look at this chattering young girl grew. *She had to have been talking to someone else, there must be another nearby,* though he couldn't smell, hear or sense anyone in the vicinity.

It had to be this way, the medieval world was wrought full of dangers, especially for dragons. Every wannabe knight or prince would proudly slay a dragon to gain a title or the maiden of his dreams. He knew if he moved, even trembled for a second, he would give up his optimal hiding position and likely be hunted to his death. If anything, his fear of being found, kept him motionless. Though no dragon should ever feel this way... in these dark ages, what dragons remained, shared stories of lost loved ones and no amount of dragon fire or retaliation, ever *truly* caused the humans to stop their onslaught, save for the rare soft-hearted soul who saw an animal rather than a monster. Few and far between, those were.

"It's okay," she spoke, as she sat down on a rock near his cheek. "I understand why you're being still and I wouldn't dare ask you to give up your hiding place, not for me. I just needed to sit down for a moment as this uphill trek can take a lot out of a girl." A moment ago, he had heard something large and metallic being laid down a few feet away and was certain it was a clanky shield, set of armor or swords, though he still wouldn't dare take a peek.

"I'm heading to Camelot. There is a wizard I've read about who has procured a stack of letters which likely lead to the mystical town of Leamore. I have been seeking this specific ogre town for quite some time now. Unfortunately, the stories I've read imply the wizard thought the letters fake and so he is going to throw the entire stack into the fire, tonight! I want to get to the letters before that happens as I believe there is a clue within one of them as to how to find the hidden town of Leamore."

The dragon's curiosity was growing as a dozen questions were pushing their way to his tongue. He knew he shouldn't move, but the girl had conflicted her story multiple times and it nagged at him. He couldn't sit quiet any longer. He was compelled to question her. Opening his eyes and raising his head as his mouth formed the words, the girl turned to watch dirt and shrubs fall to the ground as he rose.

"Why does it seem as if you are speaking of past events regarding the burning of the letters, and yet anticipate getting to them before they are burned, and what on earth is an ogre?"

"Hello, Mr. Dragon." Kyrea smiled as she nodded to him. "I hope I didn't wake you."

He looked over at the odd-shaped metallic contraption lying on the ground next to her. It wasn't armor or a weapon, but instead, it looked like two wheels connected by a seat. She wasn't reaching for it, she didn't look frightened and she wasn't running away from him. *Who is this odd girl?* He thought.

"I truly hope you don't mind my talking with you. I have read so many books about dragons, and feel like I have lived those adventures through the stories, but of all of my years, I have never been privileged enough to actually speak to a dragon. Besides seeking these letters, my main hope for traveling back in time was to satisfy my curiosity about your species."

"You seem to like dragons, though every story I know is about how humans hunt and kill us. They are afraid of us. What stories could you possibly have heard?" The dragon inquired.

"In my time… uh, kingdom, people write stories as often as birds sing songs. There are friendly dragons, flying dragons, water dragons, magical dragons, and more. These dragon stories share tales of eternal friendships, sharing hearts and souls, and protecting children from harm. The stories I have read of this era make me sad at the way they treat dragons, so I have always wanted to befriend one and tell them just how special they truly are to me, and to the world."

"Well, I appreciate that," he spoke, "though you have left yourself quite vulnerable to me, had I been hungry or untrusting of you."

"I realize that," her eyes smiled up at the beautiful seafoam green dragon, "but I wasn't worried."

"Now," the dragon began, eyes set keenly on the girl "what *do* you mean by traveling back in time?"

"Don't let her get away!" The lead knight declared with his sword held high, the other knights following close behind.

The rising sound of the knight's attack yanked the dragon from his earlier memory, back to the present scene unfolding below. He watched the girl haphazardly riding that awkward two-wheeled contraption without much concern of the armored knights behind her.

Kyrea pedaled furiously, her eyes darting across the final page of the Leamore letters. She couldn't help but marvel at her good fortune, every detail of her plan had fallen into place perfectly. She had been able to slip past the castle staff, undetected. She had entered through the kitchen while carrying a large goblet brimming with wildflowers she'd gathered along the way. Thanks to her thorough study of the kingdom's maps, that she procured in the future, she knew exactly where to find the wizard's bed-chamber. And, even more importantly, she knew he would be occupied teaching young Arthur the art of the sword. This would give her the perfect opportunity to retrieve the documents she'd come for.

Upon finding the letters in the wizard's bed-chambers, she settled down to read them. She had been skimming through the pages of Sanskrit ogre writings as a love story developed. Shared between two ogre's who had been in hiding longer than they could have ever imagined, they wrote letters to detail their love and longing to find one another. What Kyrea sought, was in the last letter of the stack. It contained the invitation spell and map to Leamore she had been seeking.

The letter claimed to contain a map, but it was only one page. And the writing was not as previous letters had been. It read more like a riddle which sent her deep into thought trying to decipher it when the wizard walked into the room.

"Who are you?" He demanded, "And what are you doing in my room?"

Kyrea sprang to her feet, taking a moment to marvel at the man she had read so much about. Shoving the last page of the Leamore letters in her side bag, she hurled the rest of the documents at him. He swatted at them, catching a few and tossing them into the fire before charging at her.

Leaping over his chair, Kyrea evaded his grasp and dashed to the far side of his desk. As he closed in, she glanced toward the open window. Without a second thought, knowing he could soon cast a spell to capture her, she leaped onto the window sill and then out into the open air. The wizard, stunned, raced to the window, but Kyrea had already landed rolling to her feet. She shot him a quick wink before sprinting toward the drawbridge.

"Thief! Stop that girl!" the wizard bellowed.

Guards pulled their swords looking for whomever it was the wizard was yelling for.

Kyrea darted to the stables, swiped off the tarp concealing her bicycle, and threw herself onto the contraption. The guards, momentarily baffled by the strange machine, hesitated just long enough for her to speed through the kingdom's gates and across the bridge. Knowing they would soon catch up, she pulled the page from her side bag and read the riddle once more, her mind racing as fast as those wheels.

> ~ *When light shines through,*
> ~ *You'll see the way*
> ~ *Open brightly, on this day*
> ~ *A realm of wonders,*
> ~ *Await your word,*
> ~ *Speak, Bukas to the third.*

Bukas is Filipino for the word "Open". She knew that from her centuries of language studies at the monastery. Say '*Open*', *to the third*, she realized she should say the word three times. She figured that part out, *but what about the light?*

Just then an arrow whizzed past her head. *Get your head in the game*, Kyrea told herself. She began peddling her bicycle faster. She rode up a hill, over it, catching air over the top and landed roughly near the bottom of the hill, dirt spraying up behind her. She was happy the move bought her a bit of distance.

From his perch atop a nearby hill, the dragon watched the distant scene unfold with concern. Kyrea seemed almost unconcerned that her lead was shortening under the relentless pursuit of the knights. Raising a piece of paper to her eyes, the rocky land and hills jostled her arm making it nearly impossible to read. Fearing for the young girl's safety, the dragon could not watch this any longer. With a roar of courage, he soared down to the field, breathing a line of dragon fire behind her to create a blazing barrier shielding her from the advancing knights.

She turned to see what he had done and then skidded to a stop. As he landed beside her, he kept switching viewpoints from the angry knights and neighing steeds, to the girl standing with this wheeled contraption, unphased and focused. Kyrea held up the paper to the setting sun, and the light illuminated a watermarked whirlpool shape which began to spin on the page. The dragon's gaze was riveted to the curious sight before him. The swirling vortex quickly expanded, engulfing the words and lifting them into the air in a shimmering display. The sunlight streaming through the paper opened what appeared to be a portal, a swirling gateway to another realm. Beyond it, a breathtaking landscape unfolded: a forest of purple trees beneath a sky of golden orange.

"It was great meeting you today, Mr. Dragon." She curtsied politely before she turned to walk into the portal. "This will be a memory I hold onto for the rest of my life."

"Does this magic take you to a place where knights don't hunt dragons?" the dragon inquired while listening to the clanking metal and angry voices of the knights just passed the fire line.

"It does" she admitted quickly knowing knights did not exist in the ogre realm. "But I cannot guarantee your safety as it is a place I have never been to, either. Ogre's can be quite brutish and I have heard tales they have a voracious appetite for human flesh, though I am certain not all of them overeat like that." Hoping this was enough information for the dragon to stay in the realm where he belonged, Kyrea took a deep breath and stepped through the portal, disappearing into the shimmering gateway. As she turned to wave at the dragon, his focus shifted back to the approaching knights, who were now shouting frantically as the flames began to wane. Their horses were reared up; their swords and shields raised in readiness for another assault.

The dragon's two hearts were beating so rapidly they lost rhythm. His eyes widened. He looked right and heard birds singing. He looked left and heard metal swords clanging on heavy metal armored shields. He looked right and saw the vibrant colors of a brand-new world. He looked left and saw fire and red and hate and death. He looked right and saw a curious young girl who was neither afraid of him nor vicious towards him, disappearing behind a bright white ring shrinking rapidly. Sure, he could fly back up to the mountains and camouflage himself, but what life is that? A life of sitting still and hiding?

He looked to the world before him. So different, so new. He could hear the flames shrinking. He could hear the knights ready for their attack. He could hear the birds singing sweetly on the other side of the portal… He did not want to look left any longer.

Desperation gripped him, and without a second thought, he thrust his wings toward the diminishing gateway. In his haste, he flew past Kyrea and crashed into a bright purple tree on the other side, the impact jolting him from his frenzied rush.

"Mr. Dragon! Are you okay?" Kyrea hurried over to the dragon; concern etched on her face. The dragon shook his head, wincing from the pain, then watched the portal finish closing behind them. With the gateway gone, he saw a continuation of this marvelous new world, Camelot was gone. His heart beats slowed as he took in the beauty. He was safe. No more knights! No more fear.

A strange new world unfolded before him. He wasn't sure if it was the impact or the surreal colors of this new realm that was causing his disorientation, but his headache was undeniable. Kyrea gently approached him, ready to offer any help she could as they both tried to make sense of their unfamiliar surroundings. She touched his head, "are you okay?"

The dragon couldn't believe his eyes, he stood, shook his wings enough to straighten them and placed them flat against his back again. The wind nearly knocked her off her feet, but she stayed upright. He took a step forward, staring at where the portal was, where he had been able to see the distant castle, and the approaching knights and now all he saw was a beautiful sea of crimson flowers amply dotted across a massive field. Surrounding them was a purple forest, trees not just with violet and burgundy leaves, but a red trunk as well. He heard water trickling in the distance, birds singing, and the wind rustling through the leaves. The smell of, *oh my*, wet soil, moldy food and musky shoes filled his sinuses. He snorted his distaste shaking his head in shock. At that moment, the shock of what he was witnessing was interrupted by the bright cheery voice of a young girl, seemingly unphased.

"You hungry? I'm hungry."

"IMMORTALITY IS NOTHING without the ability to explore magical realms." Kyrea explained to the dragon sitting next to her. "It wasn't enough to simply live forever; I had to find a way to experience a greater life." She paused as the fishing rod in her hands gave a sudden tug. Reeling in her catch, she continued her story. "When I found myself alone, at the top of the mountain, I looked out at the enormity of the world before me and took it all in. I had been saved. Yet I didn't know how."

"You have no idea who granted your wish?" The dragon inquired while staring curiously at the young girl sitting next to him. His golden eyes glistened as the medium-sized rainbow fish thrashed around on the line attempting to escape.

"Nope," Kyrea unhooked the fish and then held it up for the dragon to see. His eyes danced with excitement, as he parted his jaws in anticipation. Kyrea chuckled as she tossed the fish into his waiting mouth. With a snap of his teeth, the fish was gone, and she continued her story.

"Everyone was dying. I was terrified. I honestly didn't know what I was going to do, so I ran. I ran out of my tiny town and continued running until my legs could not continue. That's when I fell to my knees. With tears in my eyes, the world around me blurred. Surrounded by trees so tall the sunlight could not break through the canopy; I was enveloped by darkness. The wind rustled through the trees. I felt the cool air on my tear-stained cheeks. With my chest tightening and my breathing labored, I cried out, to anyone who could hear me, and I begged to live."

"And something saved you." The dragon finalized. The spikes on the top of his head stood at attention. His chin rested on his palm as he focused on the girl. She looked like any human child. About twelve years of age, beautiful, long brown hair which spiraled down her back. A nice ivory button-down shirt with rolled-up sleeves. Yet she smelled like honeysuckle and lilac with a hint of magic that he just couldn't place. *...was it Wisteria?*

"I wish I knew who or what saved me. I long to thank it for its generosity, but after all of this time, I have yet to find what it could have been." She turned to look at the dragon lying next to her. Her green eyes glistened in the midday sun. "You wouldn't know what could grant a wish like that, would you?"

"Let's see," the dragon sat up mulling over the question. His wings spread out and flapped a few times as he pondered. "A genie comes to mind."

"You're right, that was the first thing I thought of as well." Kyrea held her hands up, parallel to each other. She turned her focus onto the small open gap between them and then widened the gap to about twenty inches apart. As she did this, a small illumination appeared and began to fill the space between. She was opening a portal. A portal to one of her past memories.

The dragon watched in awe as Kyrea's memory played out like a holographic movie before him. The montage depicted her travels across the Middle East and Africa, each scene capturing her quest for answers. He saw her conversing with dozens of Genies and a handful of Djinn, (Arabic genies with immense power) all of whom shook their heads in denial. One Djinn, visibly embarrassed by his ignorance, slunk away with a scowl.

As the light of the memory dimmed, the dragon turned his gaze to the landscape before him. Across a river lay a field of golden-yellow flowers which shimmered in the sunlight, their vibrant hue reminiscent of a field of gold. The scene before him felt both enchanting and familiar, offering a moment of respite amid their adventure.

"What about fairies, leprechauns or trolls?"

Kyrea smiled at the dragon; "I have talked to many of them with no luck. I know I haven't talked to every one of them in the world, but I kind of thought they may talk amongst each other, share stories of their great adventures and good deeds."

The dragon nodded in agreeance as he continued to ponder her question. Staring into the stream as the water trickled by, the dragon listened intently to the gentle sounds of the babbling brook. The soft gurgle and occasional splash created a soothing rhythm which contrasted sharply with the earlier chaos. The dragon's mind slowly began to settle as he immersed himself in the tranquility, a calming backdrop to the bewildering new world around him. Closing his eyes with water in mind, it came to him.

"What about mermaids?"

Kyrea shook her head, "I even traveled back in time to the underwater city of Atlantis!"

"How…" the dragon paused, clearly unsure which question to ask first. She had just mentioned time travel, *again*.

Kyrea glanced up at him with a smirk. "How did I travel back in time or how did I hold my breath to swim down to Atlantis?"

"Both!" The dragon sat up, wrapped his long tail around to his front and gripped the end. Holding it against his chest like a blankie. His wide-eyed expression made it clear; both answers baffled him.

"The first one's easy," Kyrea said. "A Time Spirit helped me." She leaned back against the rock, as if that explained everything. "Of course, Time Spirits never reveal themselves to non-magical beings," she added. "Luckily, the monks taught me some variation of alchemy. Combine that with centuries of study, travel, and discovery... I guess I was just unique enough to earn an audience with one in her realm."

The dragon blinked. Kyrea continued.

"I also brought her a very rare chrono lens as a gift. I found it buried in an old antique shop. They thought it was a paper weight." Kyrea chuckled. "So, in return, she let me slip briefly back in time to visit Atlantis, it was amazing."

"And that's how you traveled back in time to medieval times as well?"

"Yes sir." Kyrea smiled. "But the moment I opened the portal to Leamore, the spell wore off."

The dragon looked as if his brain had just folded in on itself. His mouth opened, closed, then opened again. So many new terms: monks, alchemy, chrono lens, Time Spirits... and she spoke of them like they were common knowledge.

Finally, he managed one coherent question: "You mentioned monks?"

"Right," she said, nodding. "The day I was saved, I awoke at the top of a mountain surrounded by a group of Taoist Monks. They took me in, taught me their ways. But after a few decades, when they realized I wasn't aging, they began teaching me magical techniques to help me find out why."

She paused, a thoughtful moment.

"For two centuries, I studied at their side. And when their wisdom reached its end, they sent me into the world to find what they could not give."

"Decades... centuries..." the dragon scoffed, "you expect me to believe you're that old? The concept of time must be different here, right?"

"Did I not mention I am immortal?" She looked up and over her shoulder to catch his stare. "I am a thousand years old and I cannot die."

He stared at her with skepticism. It was easy to accept she was a twelve-year-old girl telling tall tales, but immortality is an entirely different concept. He stared at the young girl sitting before him. She looked young, with a smooth rounded face, innocent green eyes, long curly brown hair, rolled-up sleeves on a button-down shirt and rather intriguing looking men's trousers with external pockets, even short laced boots, which she'd later call *Hiking* boots. It was not a manner of dress he was used to seeing young maidens wear, even in the northern reaches where women ruled as queens. It helped him a little to believe her tall tales may have some truth to them. But was she telling him the *full* truth?

"So, if I breathe fire on you, you will not burn to death?" He grinned with sharp teeth.

"You would ruin my outfit and maybe singe my hair, but no, I will not die."

"That's preposterous!" The dragon stood up with indignity. "Dragon fire is the hottest most powerful fire in the world!"

The look on his face was a mix of anger and humiliation. He was truly hurt by the idea that his dragon fire wouldn't cause her to perish. "I had no intention of hurting your feelings, my friend." Kyrea stood with her hands up. "Would you like to try to burn me? I don't mind."

The dragon stared down at her, scowling and indecisive. He was befuddled. He wanted to prove her wrong and soothe his wounded pride, except she had been nothing but kind to him. He would hate to accidentally burn her to death, and yet... it was unfathomable to consider any mortal being able to survive a gust of dragon fire.

He pondered the option for a moment longer before sitting back down with a huff. "Nah," he concluded, "I'll take your word for it." He was clearly disappointed.

"No really, you can." She encouraged him. She held up her left hand, palm up to the sky. "Just ignite a small flame here in the palm of my hand."

Staring at her palm, his right brow lifted slightly. His eyes shifted from her palm to her face. She was smiling. Not at all scared or concerned. *Was she taunting him? Daring him? Did she not think he would do it?* Curiosity was working overtime. With some hesitation, the dragon cleared his throat. "Are you sure?" He finally inquired.

"Of course!" Kyrea smiled, still holding her hand out to catch the flame. Her eyes held an excitement he just couldn't grasp.

"This isn't a trick, is it?" The dragon shifted. "You aren't going to try to use my flame against me or do anything nefarious, are you?"

"Cross my heart and hope to die." She crossed her heart with the motion of her right hand while keeping her left palm up and in place.

"And you *can't* die…" the dragon winked at her.

Kyrea's expression softened into a serene smile, her eyes reflecting a deep calm. She displayed neither fear nor deceit. Instead, she looked determined.

Despite having lived for a thousand years and exploring countless lands and magical realms, she still felt there was so much more to experience. Each day brought new discoveries and thrills. With the power to travel through time, she could revisit any missed moments from the past and relive them. Add in, the ability to open realms when magical objects provided the opportunity, the idea of missing out on any of these opportunities was inconceivable to her.

"It will be fine," Kyrea assured him. She saw the hesitation in his eyes. She smiled and nodded encouragingly at him. "I promise."

Accepting her challenge, the dragon inhaled, aligned his sight to her hand and released a medium-sized flame. The small explosion frightened nearby critters which scurried and flew away. But when he returned his attention to Kyrea's hand, he was amazed to see her still holding the flame like a wick on a candle. She rolled it around her fingers like a ball and then juggled it back and forth between both of her hands. Finally, she lowered her hands to the river and let the flame extinguish.

"I have never seen a human do that. Not even the ones with powerful magic." He stared at the girl who was watching the last puff of the smoke drift away in the wind. "You truly are unique."

"I never really thought of it that way." She sat back down, her back to him. "I am just me. A young-looking girl with an amassed amount of knowledge which could fill a library ten thousand times. Who is always on the search for adventure while seeking enlightenment I may never receive."

"You may never receive?"

She turned to face the dragon, "I am a thousand years old." She spoke very surely. "The creature, entity or God that saved me all of those centuries ago, may have perished a long time ago."

"I didn't think of that."

OGRES OF IEAMORE

THE CLOUDS LOOKED LIKE PUFFS of fluffy marshmallows drifting in an ocean of a golden-yellow sky. As Kyrea watched them fly past her head, she reached out a hand to touch them. The cool, wet mist was unlike anything she had ever felt. However, the moisture of the clouds evaporated almost instantly, before her mind could fully register its presence. It was the oddest sensation actually touching a cloud.

Riding on the dragon's back, she leaned forward to keep her balance. The dragon flew so fast she could hardly keep her eyes open. Attempting to divert her eyes from the wind, she looked down to the ground.

It seemed like they were flying slow. Yet, watching the shadow of the dragon navigating over prairies, hills and trees, it felt as if they were zooming at high speed. Flying was an exhilarating experience she had not encountered in her long life.

"Are you okay back there?" the dragon asked out of curiosity for the young girl he was carrying hundreds of feet up in the sky.

"Of course," she replied.

"You are not afraid?"

"Why should I be?"

"I could drop you."

"Well, that would be exhilarating."

"Until you land..." He added.

"Even after the dragon fire, you still don't believe I am immortal, do you?" She giggled.

"If you wouldn't die, would you at least break some bones?" He inquired with a little too much enthusiasm to learn the answer to his question.

"You're a little morbid, Mr. Dragon."

He laughed aloud. "I don't mean to be."

"It's okay." Kyrea smiled, contemplating his question. Her thoughts were interrupted though when he spoke an oddly long word.

"Arloculotomous."

"Arlocu....?" Kyrea tried to respond having missed the extended part of the word as well as the reason this phrase was even being said to her.

"It's my name." He added, "Arloculotomous."

"Oh wow, that is a very nice name." She smiled trying to say it aloud. "Or-la-cu...?"

"You can call me Arlo, if that helps."

"It helps a lot." Kyrea laughed. "Do you know that Arlo means dinosaur friend?"

"What's a dinosaur?"

Kyrea shook her head. Maybe one day she would try to explain to him about the distant past and the era of dinosaurs, but maybe, dinosaurs are just dragons from a much further past than him?

Returning her thoughts back to the present conversation, she spoke his name carefully to prove to him, that it was important to her to know his full name, even though she couldn't easily pronounce it, "Arla-Q-lotta-mouse."

"Pretty close." The dragon chuckled.

There was silence for a moment, save for the wind rushing past her ears and the occasional beat of his enormous wings. Kyrea turned her thoughts inward, deciding to answer his earlier question about immortality.

"I've never broken a bone," she said quietly. "Though... I suppose I've never put myself in a position where one might break."

"You're telling me in a thousand years, you've never had an accident?" the dragon scoffed.

She didn't answer right away.

Arlo waited, watching her out of the corner of his eye. After a long pause, curiosity got the better of him. "Wwwweeeeellll?"

"Sorry, I was thinking" She responded. "I do not recall any major accidents. Yes, I've been alive for a thousand years, and I guess most people would have a lot more memories of the bad times, but I choose to always remember the good times. And there have been so many of them there's just not any room for the bad times."

"That's a good way of looking at life," Arlo said with a smile. Another quiet moment passed before he spoke again. "Do you feel pain?"

"Yes, of course, she responded quickly. "You watched me stand up earlier today and bump my head on that low tree branch."

"Right!" He smiled recalling how he laughed at her. A few minutes later, he slowed his flight and then announced, "We're coming up to the town."

Kyrea looked ahead to see the town of Leamore coming into sight. She was very much looking forward to meeting Gozan the Ogre. She heard he had once conned a princess of her diary, and that diary was said to have contained a sketch of a map which could lead her to her next set of answers.

As they approached the town of Leamore Kyrea stood and leapt from the dragon's back while in mid-flight. Turning his head just slightly in absolute shock, he nearly lost his train of thought and had to refocus on his flight. He stretched out his hind legs preparing for his landing and landed as quickly as he could. As soon as he was safe on the ground he spun around in order to go find Kyrea. When he did, he saw the girl nonchalantly walking towards him. Not even a scratch on her knees.

"Seriously?" His jaw dropped open. "I was flying at a good eighty miles per hour when I slowed for my landing! I was about twenty-five feet off the ground. At that speed and height, you should have at least twisted an ankle!"

"Are you disappointed?" Kyrea cocked her head to the side with a furrowed brow.

"Well no," he back peddled, "but I *am* shocked."

"I told you I was immortal."

"I guess I just didn't believe it." He confirmed.

"Well believe it," she smiled coyly.

His eyes followed her as she passed him, then he began to follow her down the path. "Why didn't you wait for me to land?"

"Honestly, we hadn't discussed you landing, so I assumed you would just take off after dropping me. I didn't expect you to stick around."

"Should I leave" Arlo asked with a little too much emotion.

"Oh no! Not if you don't want to. I just didn't want to assume you were going to stick with me. You are free now, to explore the world."

"Yes, but this is your world. I don't know anything about it."

"Well, it's not MY world, it's an Ogre world, but I understand what you are saying."

They continued their short trek towards Leamore's entrance, talking, and when they arrived, the dragon stopped walking. "This is as far as I'm going to go."

"I understand." She turned to face him. "Ogres are not a friendly bunch." She confirmed.

"Actually, they kind of smell bad." His nose crinkled up at the pungent aroma emanating from the town. "A dragon's sense of smell is quite acute."

"Is it?" She asked as she sniffed the air, not smelling much of anything. Then she sniffed her wrist. "I hope my scent hasn't offended you."

"It has not," he answered quickly. "I'm kind of intrigued about it actually. Most humans have a pungent odor that I don't like. But you, you smell sweet, like honeysuckle and lilacs."

"Thank you," she replied, though she hadn't been anywhere near honeysuckle or lilacs for a very long time. She wondered how she would have that smell, especially since she didn't smell it herself.

She waved goodbye to the dragon and continued walking towards town. That's when she heard Arlo call out one last thing. "If you need anything, just whistle. You can whistle, can't you?"

She turned around, placed two fingers; her thumb and index finger, into her mouth and blew hard. The volume of the sound she whistled was so loud, every bird within a 10-acre distance took off from the treetops.

When the dragon's attention pulled from the birds in flight to find the young girl again, she had already entered through the gates of the town. "What a curious young girl," he murmured.

Walking into town, Kyrea caught the attention of just about every on-looker within eyeshot. She gazed upon the dark stone buildings while reading any signs she could spot. The Sanskrit-like writing was nearly illegible but she was able to translate enough to know the town had a medic, a brewery, a textile shop, an apothecary and something that passed as an old-country store. Spotting a bushel of peaches in the window, Kyrea climbed up the steps and sashayed through the door.

The pungent aroma of body odor and rotting fruit smacked her senses but she refused to show her distaste by scrunching her nose. Instead, she went over to the bushel of peaches and began digging for one where the fuzz was natural to the peach and not a blueish-gray mold. Picking a peach with only minor bruising, she took it up to the counter and inquired about the price with the large male ogre standing there staring at her with shock.

Looking the young girl up and down he was bewildered why such a nice young thing would have walked willingly into their unwelcoming town. "One shekel." He responded gruffly.

Kyrea pulled a tree leaf from her shirt pocket and slid it onto the counter. "This ought to cover it." She spoke as a puff of smoke escaped from under her hand. When she lifted her palm, she exposed a bright golden leaf sparkling in the sunlight.

The ogre's eyes widened. He gawked at the gold leaf, picked it up, and eyed it carefully noting the veins and intricate design. He then placed it on the side of his mouth and bit down on it with his teeth. Looking at it again he spotted where his tooth imprinted the cool, soft gold. "This leaf's solid gold!"

"Yes sir." Kyrea acknowledged.

"Um... do you need change?" He shifted.

"No thank you. Keep the change. Mr..." She trailed off hoping he'd provide his name.

"Thao" he offered his name.

Smiling, she took a bite of the peach. The juices were sweet and the meat of the peach was soft. She chewed and swallowed, then wiped her chin from the extra juice which ran down. The ogre just stood there staring at her so Kyrea took this moment to ask a question. "Do you know of any tales about magical creatures that could grant wishes in this world?"

"You mean like genies?" Kyrea nodded while chewing. He thought on it, then answered. "I've only heard about genies but never knew of any. I don't think I've ever heard of anything else that grants wishes. Why?" he inquired.

"Just curious." She was about to take another bite of peach when she paused, "Would you know where I could find Gozan the Ogre?"

"It's just Gozan. You don't need to add 'the Oger' part when you are talking to another Ogre."

"Right! My mistake. Only Trolls require the 'Troll' to be added after every name."

"Actually, that is primarily for the Norwegian Trolls. Trolls of the Springshire Realm aren't quite as proper." Thao the Ogre admitted.

"Springshire. Right." Kyrea placed that realm into memory before turning her attention back to Thao. "So Gozan, I can find him where?"

"Follow the road down to the stalls, make a left and then four clicks." The ogre pointed his directions.

Kyrea smiled, curtsied, gave her thanks and then took another bite of the over-sweet peach as she walked out the door. The ogre stared as she left and watched until she walked out of view before turning his attention back to the gold leaf in his hand. A smile spread across his face as he slid it into his pocket.

Following his directions, Kyrea finished her peach, tossed the seed into a nearby ditch, then moseyed down the road to a dark stone hut covered in moss and vines. Just inside his walking path she kneeled down, untied her shoes and then knotted them together. Hanging them from a low tree branch, almost in the way of the pathway, she turned and continued to the front door in her socks. Following the stench of burnt soup and sage she stopped just shy of the welcome mat. She leaned forward, knocked on the door and then leaned back.

"Go away!" a gruff voice bellowed from inside.

"I'm looking for Gozan. Are you, he?"

"Please wait on the welcome mat. I'll be right there." Just then Kyrea watched the welcome mat disappear as it fell down into a deep dark well. She heard laughter from inside the hut as the trap door closed back up again. She stood there quietly and waited as the sounds of feet shuffled across the dirt floor and neared the door.

When the door opened, she saw a large ogre standing there with another welcome mat in his hand. His smile faded to a scowl when he saw her staring at him. "Why weren't you on the mat?"

"I know ogres well enough to not fall for that silly trick," she smiled coyly.

He stared at her for a moment, his eyes blinked twice. "What do you want?" He grumbled.

"Answers."

"You might as well come inside. It's too bright out here." He turned leaving the door open and proceeded to walk back across the hut to his chair. Kyrea stepped over the welcome mat and closed the door behind her. As the light left the dank room, she focused her eyes to watch the ogre plop down on his chair and toss his large, calloused feet onto his ottoman. He grabbed his drink from the side table and took a sip as he watched Kyrea slowly make her way across the room, eyeing everything she saw.

His hut looked small on the outside, but inside it was deep. He had long strands of peppers, and strings of garlic cloves, dangling down the walls. Mushrooms were growing on a dirt pile next to his chair and a collection of tea cups on a bookshelf that looked to be in a kitchen, of sorts. He even had a collection of shoes, all different colors, styles, and sizes, piled high as a car by his bed. That seemed about the best place to start.

"That sure is an eclectic assortment of shoes you have there." Kyrea pointed to the pile.

"You can't have them!" He barked while snagging a mushroom from the pile by his chair. He bit off the head of the mushroom and then threw the stem back onto the pile.

"I wouldn't even consider." Kyrea smiled as she walked over to his table. "I know how much ogres cherish their collections. I was just commenting how great it was."

"Oh… thank you." He grumbled as he turned to admire his trove. "Which one is your favorite?"

Kyrea glanced up from the table and back over to the pile of shoes. She walked over there, looking carefully at each shoe. She was seeking a specific style and wasn't sure she would find it. She picked through the top a bit then followed a small avalanche of shoes to the floor. That's where she found it, one shoe at least. She picked it up and gushed with excitement. "Oh this one! This one is fabulous!"

The ogre stood from his chair and snatched the shoe from Kyrea's hand. He looked at it closely, sniffed the inside and then smiled. "This one is very special. It is one of my favorites!"

"Oh, well I am glad I found it for you. Why is it your favorite? The color? The style?"

"The girl I got this from! She was pretty, like you. But with yellow hair."

"What happened to her, to want to leave such a wonderful shoe behind?"

"I scared her," he laughed. "I was sitting in a mud pit, cooling off you know." He looked at Kyrea to make sure she understood why he was there. She nodded knowingly like that made the most sense of anything, so he continued. "Anyways, that's when I saw her, sitting in a small chariot being pulled by a white horse. She was staring at some brown thing, not paying attention, so I jumped up and scared her."

Kyrea began to laugh with him as if they had been buddies for years sharing the same funny story. As he continued telling the story their laughter got louder and more rambunctious.

"When the horse stopped and backed up, the jolt threw her forward out of her seat. When the horse took off running, the momentum threw her back into her seat where her feet flipped up over her head."

Kyrea fell to the floor, holding her tummy she was laughing so hard. Then, with exaggerated flair, she mimicked the move the ogre had described, theatrically acting out the scene so he could relive the memory. The performance softened his cautious demeanor, drawing him back to that humorous moment in time while keeping his thoughts distracted from the young girl standing before him, still a mystery as to why she was here or what she wanted.

"That's right!" The ogre continued his story. "She flipped backward so fast her left shoe was tossed from her foot. It, and the brown thing she was staring at, landed by my feet as the horse and carriage took off down the road."

"That is hilarious!" Kyrea laughed as she stood back up, placing her hand on the table. When she did a couple of dishes tumbled to the floor. "I'm so sorry." She apologized, hoping the action didn't pull the ogre from his funny memory.

"It's okay. Hey, there's the brown thing." He reached to the table and lifted up a brown leather-bound diary. The gold filigree around the edges caught Kyrea's attention. This had to be the diary she was looking for! "Oh my, what an odd-looking brown thing." She spoke as she reached to take the diary from his hands and look at it.

The ogre pulled it away from her reaching hand and held it up by his shoulder. "What are you doing?"

"I just wanted to see it." She smiled.

"Why?"

"Curiosity is all. I mean, that shoe was so pretty, pearly white with the oddest high heel, and then this odd brown book, both came from the same yellow-haired girl. It doesn't fit, does it?"

"No…" the ogre agreed while bringing the book back down towards Kyrea's extended hand. She almost had her hand on it when he paused. Staring at Kyrea carefully. "What did you call this?"

"Hmm?" She stalled, raising her eyebrows.

"How did you know this was a book?"

"I can see it is." Kyrea smiled brightly hoping the ogre didn't pick up a whiff of her fear.

"Why did you say you were here, again?"

"I didn't."

Just then the ogre seemed to grow an extra two feet as he leaned over the young girl with an angry scowl on his face. He was trying to frighten her but Kyrea wasn't fazed. She just stepped past him and sat down on his chair placing her feet up on his ottoman. He turned to look defiantly at the girl who dared to sit in his chair and growled loudly.

"I'm not trying to upset you sir. I was just told by so many ogres your shoe collection was the best and this is the place I needed to visit."

"My shoes? The best collection?" His frown turned upside down. With a smile spreading across his face, he leaned up against his table with dreamy eyes. A few moments passed before his distrust edged in again. "Who told you about my collection?"

"Everyone I asked!" The medic looked so envious as he described those purple shoes you have there. But it was Thao the shop owner who suggested I come see you directly."

"Thao told you about my collection? Why?"

"As you can see, I have no shoes. I went into his store to find something but he suggested I would have better luck here." Kyrea spoke as she pulled a green tree leaf from her pocket and placed it on the arm of the chair. A puff of smoke escaped from under her hand as she lifted it and picked up the bright gold leaf that now sat there. "I'm more than happy to pay for the shoes of course." She held up the gold leaf for Gozan to see. His eyes widened. As he started to reach for the leaf, she pulled it back to her shoulder. "Of course, I must find a good pair of shoes first."

Gozan couldn't take his eyes off the shiny gold leaf she held in her hand. "Sure. You can pick a pair of shoes." He reached for the leaf but she kept it just out of his reach as she returned to the shoe pile and picked up the beautiful high heel which belonged to the princess. "Do you have the matching shoe that goes with this?"

"No I don't." Gozan frowned. He really wanted the golden leaf. He began trying to think of what he could sell her for it. He remembered her interest in the brown book. He reached for it and started to hand it to her. "I could sell you this book."

"That is so generous, and I would love to take this off your hands, but I need a pair of shoes. That is the whole reason I am here, after all." She lifted her right leg and wiggled her socked toes. The ogre looked at the toes for a moment and then returned his gaze to the golden leaf.

"Tell you what," she smiled, "since you don't have a complete set of these really pretty shoes, what if I settle for the purple pair there and you throw in the brown book thing with them? That would at least be worth this gold, right?"

"That sounds fair." The ogre snatched the leaf from her hands as she took the book from him and placed it under her arm. She reached for the purple shoes with her right hand, passed them to her left, and gripped them tightly. As she reached for the door with her now-free hand, the ogre finished biting the gold, confirming it was real.

"It's real!" He proclaimed.

"Of course it is." She opened the door letting the bright daylight inside. He shielded his eyes from the light but noticed how the gold sparkled in his hand. He was so happy with his sale... until the door closed. As soon as the darkness enveloped the room, he looked over at his colorful shoe pile and suddenly missed the purple pair. It wasn't the same without them. As per any ogre's short attention span, he immediately forgot how happy he was with the gold leaf and decided, instead, to go after the girl.

Kyrea was already running down the path. She grabbed her shoes from the tree and slid them over her neck like a tie, letting one dangle from either side. She was just about to turn the corner when she heard the ogre throw open his door and call out after her. "You girl, stop right there!"

"Typical fickle ogre," Kyrea mumbled under her breath as she picked up speed. Gozan hot on her trail, again, yelled at her, "You stole my shoes!"

"I did not!" she yelled back but it didn't stop nearby neighbor ogres from deciding to get in on the chase. Now Kyrea had three ogres chasing her down the road and for no good reason. The brown-leather book was securely pressed against her chest with her elbow, a pair of purple shoes clutched between her fingers in her left hand, and her own shoes dangling over her neck, she took the free hand of her right arm, placed two fingers into her mouth and whistled as hard as she could.

The sound caught the attention of a few ogres in town and upon seeing their fellow ogres chasing this young girl, they decided to run towards her. Four ogres to the front of her, at least three behind her and all of them closing in.

Just then, a dark shadow swooped in from overhead. Knowing the dragon had arrived, Kyrea leaped up into his paw and was lifted up to the sky. As they flew over the town, she spotted Thao, the shop owner as he stepped out of his store to see what all of the commotion was about. When he looked up at the dragon flying overhead, Kyrea dropped the purple shoes into his hands.

She watched as the other ogres stopped, all except Gozan who ran up to Thao and snatched the purple shoes out of his hands as if Thao was suddenly the thief. "These are mine!" Gozan declared angrily and then turned to leave as if he had already forgotten about the girl.

"Silly ogres with their short-term memory."

She then slid the diary into her side bag and began putting her shoes back on as Arlo flew out of sight of the town.

A Variation of Alchemy

That evening, after Kyrea had collected some twigs and set the wood in a makeshift campfire. Arlo blew a small flame from his nostril and then watched as she sat down by the roaring fire. After dinner and some rest, she reached over to the brown book she had acquired and opened it to read through and consume what information it contained.

"I didn't realize you were going to steal from the ogres." The dragon proclaimed in a huff.

"Steal?" Kyrea looked up, her eyes and mouth wide-open expressing her shock, "I did no such thing! Did you *not* see the purple shoes I had were returned to Gozan?"

"That book?" Arlo alluded to.

"I paid for it – as well as the purple shoes, I'll have you know," Kyrea added while pulling a tree leaf from her pocket to show Arlo.

"I may be a dragon but leaves literally grow on trees. They are not forms of payment."

"They may not be worth anything in this form, but with a little alchemy they are worth their weight in gold," Kyrea smirked.

"Alchemy?" You know how to turn objects into gold?" The dragon was clearly impressed.

"Of course," Kyrea shrugged with a smirk, tucking the leaf back into her pocket. "A bit of focus, a bit of intent. Alchemy is the art of understanding the hidden structure of things, the way matter can change. It's about persuading elements to become something more."

The dragon narrowed his eyes thoughtfully.

"And besides," Kyrea added, "ogres have a short-term memory and magical creatures aren't obsessed with currency like humans are. We appreciate beauty. Sparkle. The story behind the shine."

Arlo nodded in agreeance, resting his chin on his front paws. As his eyelids grew heavy, he drifted off to the sound of paper turning in the distance.

The next morning the dragon opened his eyes to see Kyrea asleep, her head lying on the pages of the book. He stood up, stretched, and looked around. The campfire had gone out hours ago. There was a light dew settled on top of all of the foliage and grass and there was a light fog lifting from the nearby water. He stretched his arms and wings, then shook his wings to break up all of the spider webs which had collected overnight.

The commotion startled nearby bunnies who scurried off and the sound caught Kyrea's ears. With a deep inhale, the young girl began to stir. Stretching her arms up she slowly opened her eyes.

"Sleep well?" He asked.

"Not much." Kyrea closed the book and placed it on the log next to her. "The princess wrote everything down. From what she ate every morning, to what she wore, to the servants who bugged her, to her tutors that wouldn't let her go out and play. She is quite spoiled." Kyrea detailed what she had read.

"Did you find any reference to what you are looking for?" The dragon picked up the small diary between his two claws and raised it to his nose. He sniffed it, but it smelled like Ogre's feet. He dropped it back to the ground while giving a good snort through his nostrils.

Kyrea watched the diary land on the ground and was grateful it didn't bounce into the ashy embers left over from the campfire. "She did mention the day her tutor tried teaching her about a legendary magician who was instrumental in helping her great-grandfather, the previous king, retrieve some magical sword from a large rock. But I have already learned of that story."

"Is that where you want to go next?" Arlo shifted his seated position.

"Unfortunately, I do believe that is going to be a dead end for the quest." Kyrea stood and walked over to the dragon. She placed her hand on his, the claw of his massive appendage larger than her entire forearm. "I'd much rather know what you would like to do today. We can go anywhere you want."

"Me?" The dragon was befuddled. He hadn't expected the girl to even ask. He expected to be used for his flight, fire or strength, or attacked by knights but never asked what he would like to do. "I… I don't know." He admitted visually bewildered. "I usually just hang out in a nearby cave until night."

"And do what?"

"Sleep."

"But you slept all night. When do you hunt, what do you eat?"

"I wouldn't stop you from pulling some more fish from the river with that stick and line of yours."

"Oh, of course we'll eat first, but then afterward, we should do something fun."

"Fun." he smiled, then pondered the word, knowing it meant enjoyment but having experienced so little of it in his life. "I agree… like what?"

"Let's see." Kyrea looked around at the nearby mountains, forest and river. While this may be the Ogre Realm, and the colors of the sky and trees were anything but normal to her eyes, the terrain seemed familiar to her. If the trees would have been green and the hills a royal blue…. One of her favorite places could have been just over the horizon. With that place in mind, she decided where they would go next. "I'd like to take you to Yorkshire Moors. I know of a beautiful little garden we could hang out in."

"Sounds good to me!"

GARDEN AT YORKSHIRE MOORS

AFTER THE DRAGON CONSUMED a
fish breakfast and Kyrea ate a handful of berries, they
were on their way. Soaring through the sky, Arlo was
heading in the direction she pointed when he felt her
legs grip tighter to his back. Peaking around and
glancing at her through his peripheral vision, he
noticed her rubbing the palms of her hands together.

She closed her eyes, whispered a few words
under her breath and then slowly widened the gap
between her hands. A small light appeared and it kept
growing. When it was about the size of a watermelon,
she shot it forward past the dragon's head and out into
the path he was flying. A portal opened before them
and Arlo's first instinct was to slow down and swerve

to avoid it. Yet he could hear Kyrea declaring proudly, "It's safe! Fly inside!"

So far, she had been trustworthy. So far, they seemed to be friends, but at this moment, a level of trust was being expected that he wasn't sure she had earned yet. She looked young and innocent but he had met witches who could look like that. She had magic but hadn't used it much. She claimed to have bought the book and yet the ogres thought she was stealing from them... granted their memories are short...

"I know you don't trust me yet," she interjected into his thoughts, "and the last portal took you from a rather dismal existence, but I promise it will be fine. Besides, if it is not, you can eat me when we get there." Arlo realized this was a good answer so he continued to fly into the open portal.

As soon as they crossed the bright white threshold, the temperature cooled. It went from a warm 90 degrees to a cool 75 degrees in an instant. His scales compressed as if he were shivering, and it took his eyes a moment to realize they were now flying through a bright white cloud. When they came out the other side, the terrain had changed drastically.

There was an old-tyme country town surrounded by lush green hills speckled with green trees. This world looked just like the medieval world he left. "Will the humans see me?" Arlo panicked as he swerved up and to the right and ducked within a cloud, then bolted upwards to fly above it.

"Probably," Kyrea acknowledged, "but the people down there haven't seen a dragon in a very long time. If they admitted to someone they just saw a dragon, they would be laughed at. So you have nothing to worry about. Head northwest just a tad towards the wooded area, then land in the clearing just on the other side."

Arlo shifted his direction but spoke nothing. Kyrea could sense he was conflicted. "It's okay Arlo, the estate over there only has one human, and she's an old friend. She would never hurt you."

Soaring just above the tree tops, the windspeed shifted as if being blocked. The effect caused just enough drag to slow his descent. As Arlo came in for his landing, it was much softer than before, almost stealth-like. Once his claws sank into the ground, he quickly shifted backward into the woods so he could blend into the green trees.

Kyrea hopped down and walked over to face him. "Arlo, I can sense you are scared, but I promise, this place is perfectly safe."

He wouldn't look at her, his eyes kept darting to and fro, all around the area, keeping a lookout for danger. From the woods, was a clearing, a bunch of pathways with flowering bushes on either side. About

50 yards away was a rounded area with a tall wall, completely encapsulated by vines. And past that, another set of trees, more paths and some beautifully shaped plants framing a quaint country house. If Arlo hadn't been so scared, he would have found the property beautiful.

"We're going just over there, within the vine-covered wall." Kyrea pointed.

Now Arlo was convinced she was trying to trap him! He didn't know why, he didn't know what he was going to do, but he was certain he needed to defend himself. He breathed out a strong flame of fire into the clearing. Birds, bunnies, deer and foxes all ran, flew and scurried away.

"Arlo, please trust me." She placed her hand on his claw. "Would it help if I made you invisible?"

Arlo paused.

He thought about it for a moment.

He glanced at her with one eyebrow raised.

"You can do that?"

"I would do anything to get you to trust me again." He looked into her eyes which were glistening with tears. "This is such a beautiful place, I just wanted to share it with you."

He looked out at the clearing. No knights on horses. No cannon fire. No Kings trumpets sounding. *Maybe it was safe?* He pondered.

"You can make me invisible?" He stared at her inquisitively. "How?"

"Your scales can be made to be reflective like a mirror or a still body of water. It would be temporary, and primarily only work if you were still or moving very slowly." She exclaimed. Turning around, she spotted a nearby turtle and reached for it. Placing it by a tree stump near Arlo, she rubbed her hands together, whispered a few words and opened her hands towards the turtle, a mystical light enveloped it. A moment later the turtle was gone.

Arlo's eyes widened. "Where did the turtle go?"

"He's still there." She tapped the turtle's shell. With a hiss and a small buck from his back legs, the turtle moved. A sparkle like you would see shimmering off of the top of a body of water when the sunlight was shining just right, displayed the invisible turtle. Arlo couldn't believe his eyes.

They watched the turtle as it slowly stuck its head out of its shell, looked both ways and then proceeded to advance down the path. While he *could* be seen when he was moving, it was as if it was a clear blur. When a bird flew down to check on the blurry item, the turtle stopped, drew his head into his shell and became completely still. When there was no motion, he was completely invisible again. It was the most amazing thing Arlo had ever seen!

"You can do that to me?"

"I can!" Kyrea smiled. "This way you can feel at ease knowing no one can see you."

Arlo stared into her eyes. She seemed to be telling the truth. She seemed so trustworthy. How could this girl make him feel this way? With a deep sigh, he closed his eyes and nodded. "Okay."

After Arlo had been made invisible, he felt much more comfortable in this world. He flew up into the sky and checked the surroundings. There was no one around for miles. The land was quite beautiful, and upon flying over the walled-in area Kyrea wanted to go into, he realized it was just a very over-grown and lusciously floral garden. He flew around it a few times, like a dog would turn in circles many times before lying down, and then he landed on the top of the wall, wrapping his long tail around the uppermost edge of the structure.

A few moments later he watched Kyrea as she walked in through a hidden door covered in vines. "Isn't this place beautiful?" She inhaled with her arms outstretched. She walked over to a concrete bench and sat down. "I used to come here to think."

She looked up at Arlo, or what would have been the dragon… if she could see him.

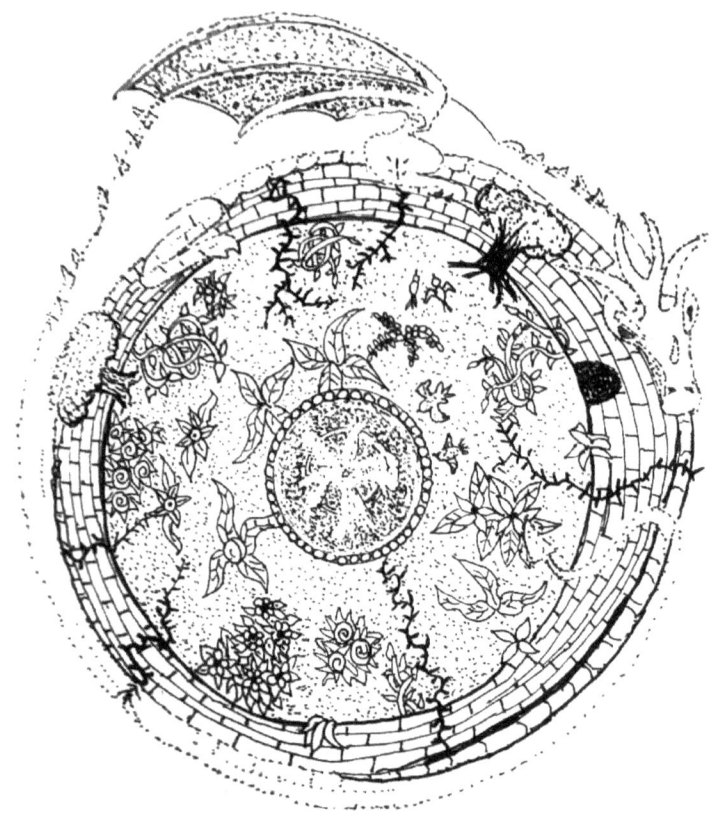

"A long time ago this garden was overrun by plants and vines. It had been neglected for years. But one day, a young lady named Mary discovered it. She worked so hard to clean it up and make it beautiful. It was her hard work, beautiful innocence and the beauty of this garden brought the entire household happiness again during a very sad time."

"That is a beautiful story, but it seems the garden has gotten overrun with vines again." Arlo noted. Kyrea looked up to see a little shimmer as he spoke. She smiled. Jumping to her feet, she walked over to an archway heavily covered by climbing vines. When she came out the other side she had two large bunches of black grapes. She bit one grape off a bunch in her right hand and held the bunch in her left hand up for Arlo. The dragon opened his mouth and she tossed it up. He caught it in his mouth and bit down. As the juice from the grapes gushed in his mouth he vocalized a load, "Mmmm!"

"Right?" She added. "This time of year, the Mustang grapes are plentiful and oh so sweet."

"So sweet!" Arlo exclaimed.

Kyrea then walked down the path to a large tree. She pointed up to the light green fruit. "Those are pears. They're like apples but softer."

Arlo reached over, picked a pear and dropped it to Kyrea, then grabbed another and popped it in his mouth. As he crunched away at the soft fruit, he watched Kyrea take a bite and walk a little further down the path. "This is a cherry bush. Cherries are really good but sometimes can be tart." She watched Arlo snatch a handful and pop them into his mouth. When he bit down on a cherry seed he flinched.

"I'm sorry. I meant to mention, cherries have seeds." Kyrea popped one in her mouth, chewed around the seed, and then spit it out into a nearby mulch pile. Arlo watched, grimacing, and then, reluctantly, swallowed the seeds. He briefly considered spitting them out like little projectiles to see how far they would go. He still might try that later, but for now, he was focused on not drawing attention to his presence.

His gaze kept bouncing around the garden, unsure of his surroundings. Though beautiful, the tranquil setting made him uneasy. He always had a nagging fear a knight might jump out from behind a bush and attack him. His heart raced as his eyes darted over the dark shadows and thick bushes, but then... he froze. A distant silhouette—crouching, waiting. The broad shoulders, the angular knee bent in preparation, a raised arm poised to strike.

For a heartbeat, Arlo sat still, his mind racing, ready to spring into action. His body tensed, and the dragon inside him stirred. He considered unleashing a burst of flame, but then the wind shifted. The trees swayed just enough to reveal that the "knight" was simply a pile of rocks, a random heap haphazardly stacked in the corner. Arlo's heart slowed, his tension melting into embarrassment. He exhaled loudly, shaking his head. *Just my imagination*, he thought.

"Something wrong?" Kyrea asked, glancing up from the fountain.

Arlo shook his head dismissively, half-smiling. "Those rocks over there… they almost look like a crouching knight ready to attack," he mused aloud.

She paused. A small smirk tugged at her lips, and the twinkle in her eyes grew. The tone of her voice shifted, light and playful.

"Well, that reminds me of the time I misplaced a rock monster," she said, letting the words hang in the air, her eyes watching him carefully, as though waiting for him to bite on the story.

Arlo's eyebrow lifted in disbelief. He shot her a sidelong glance, a mix of sarcasm and amusement in his tone. "Really?" he asked, clearly skeptical. "How does one lose a rock monster?"

"**M**ISPLACING A ROCK MONSTER may not seem like an easy feat to accomplish, but you'd be shocked how they camouflage themselves!" Kyrea looked up at Arlo then winked, "Although, maybe you would." She laughed.

As Arlo was listening to Kyrea tell him what had to be a tall tale about misplacing a large rock monster, he watched a bird fly down and land at the nearby fountain. The bird looked into the concrete fountain but seemed to not like what it saw. He then watched the bird fly up to the spout where the water was just barely flowing and inspect what was trickling out. The bird seemed to conclude that the water wasn't clean enough to drink and flew away without quenching its thirst. Arlo stood up and made his way over to the fountain to inspect it.

"So anyways, as soon as we crossed through the threshold of the portal Raken disappeared!"

"Raken?" Arlo glanced over at Kyrea.

"The rock monster. Though Raken didn't like the term monster, he felt more like a heavy soul."

Arlo smiled as he listened, yet dipped his claw into the dark green water of the fountain, pulling out a chunk of heavy algae plant with it.

"So I spent the next two months searching for him! I searched everywhere. There were all of these people in the realm and I kept hearing stories of odd rock avalanches which just appeared on a roadway but were oddly gone by the time the person procured the proper heavy equipment or tools to break up the rock into smaller pieces and remove it. That's what led me to him. I went from town to town until one day I heard two neighbors yelling at each other…"

Kyrea stopped talking when she noticed Arlo's claw full of algae gunk. He scrunched his nose and let the stuff plop back into the thick green water.

She stood up and walked over to the fountain. Sitting down on the ledge. She then placed her hand in the water and swirled it around. An aroma of muck and dirt permeated the air. "Oh my, that is some nasty-smelling water, isn't it?"

"Can you clean it?" Arlo inquired, though he was thinking she would use some sort of alchemy to accomplish said task.

"Of course, I can!" She walked around to the other side of the fountain, pulled what looked like a giant straw from a cabinet, and placed it over the spout of the fountain. The other end was laid just over the side of the fountain wall, so within a few seconds, the water was being redirected out of the fountain and into the garden. She then pulled a large bucket and brush from the cabinet. Arlo was confused.

"What are you doing?"

"Cleaning the fountain."

"I thought you would just rub your hands together, whisper some magic words, and the water would just turn clear," Arlo admitted.

Kyrea laughed. "What fun would that be?"

"It would be a whole lot easier."

"The best feeling in the world is seeing the benefits and rewards of your hard work."

"Did you learn that from the monks?"

Kyrea thought about it for a moment, then shook her head. "But I also learned this one from the monks: Do today what must be done. Who knows what tomorrow will bring."

"What does that mean?" Arlo asked.

"See a need and fill it."

"Now you seem to be speaking in riddles."

Kyrea rolled up her pants and unbuttoned her top. Arlo glanced away but peaked just in time to see she was wearing a tank top underneath. He blushed but then smiled it away. She then kicked off her shoes and stepped barefoot into the fountain. With the bucket in one hand, she began retrieving the coins and rocks that were on the bottom of the fountain.

Arlo watched the intriguing young girl get dirtier than he could stomach. She collected the coins in the bucket and threw the stones into a small pile outside of the fountain. After a while, the pile of rocks reminded Arlo of the story she was telling him earlier. "That reminds me, did you ever find Raken, the Rock Monster?"

"Oh my!" Kyrea laughed, "I am surprised you remembered the story I was telling. Most people pay so little attention when someone is talking, that they can't remember what you were saying. I am thoroughly impressed."

"Well dragons have good memories, and love to listen, especially to interesting stories."

"Let's see… where was I?" Kyrea asked as she leaned up against the center of the fountain, her algae-green fingers strumming her chin as she tried to remember where she left off.

"You spent two months searching for him and then you got a lead."

"Right! So, the neighbors were standing on opposite sides of their fence. Both yelling at one another. The one guy was accusing the neighbor on the other side, of maliciously leaving these large stones on his driveway. He was pointing out the landscaping he was doing. The other neighbor was adamantly denying it but couldn't answer the question of where the large boulders came from."

Arlo continued listening as she detailed the story. He visualized the scene taking place. He envisioned a short white picket fence separating two angry men currently yelling at each other. Then he saw a large pile of boulders sprawled out across the first guy's driveway. He could only imagine what was being said, but he saw the one man cross over the fence to storm across the yard and point to a large pile of dirt next to a hole in his neighbor's grass.

"You're trying to tell me this big hole was just dirt and you didn't toss those boulders over the fence to get rid of them?"

"Toss them? They are way too large to pick up!"

"My wife said you had heavy equipment and trucks over here yesterday. They could have done it."

"But you came home last night, you drove on the driveway. Look, your car is on the other side of the rocks." The neighbor pointed to the pile of stones behind the neighbor's car.

"And that's why I am angry! Your rocks are blocking my ability to leave!"

"But they aren't *MY* rocks!"

"Who's else could they be?"

As Kyrea kept telling her story, Arlo imagined her walking up the driveway. She walked by the bickering men in the other yard and looked closely at the large boulders. She walked around, inspecting them, and then located a few smaller round pebbles at the end of some of the larger stones. She reached out and tickled them, and that's when Raken sat up laughing. "How did you know?" He chuckled.

"I would know your chubby little toes anywhere." She helped him get to his feet. Dust and debris fell off of him as he stood, towering over her. "Are you ready to go now?" Kyrea pointed to the mountain range housing the cave with the magical opening that they came through.

"Aw, I guess so. But this has been such a fun realm. These hoo-mans get angry so quickly."

"That they do." Kyrea acknowledged as they walked away. Once they were out of sight, the bickering on the other side of the fence continued to escalate. Arlo imagined the remainder of the scene as the neighbor walked the other neighbor back to the fence, gripping hold of his shirt collar. He pointed to where the pile of boulders had been sitting and without looking, declared, "You WILL get these removed today or I will…"

"They're gone!" The neighbor gasped.

The other man whipped his head around and stared with a shocked face at the dirt and debris which remained where that huge pile of rocks had been. He couldn't figure out how the rocks had been removed so quickly, or how he didn't hear the tractor trucks lifting and moving them, but he was glad the stones were gone.

He released the neighbor's shirt and smoothed it a bit before he added one last thing to their *fight*. "And I expect the rest of this dirt cleaned up by the time I get home tonight!" He then turned to leave feeling vindicated, while the other neighbor began looking around for where the boulders just may have disappeared to. *It's like they just walked away...*

"That is hilarious, Kyrea!" Arlo laughed as the girl resumed her coin collecting. The water in the fountain had almost all drained out, but there was still a lot of work to do. Algae plants and gunk were thick in places. When Kyrea was finished with the collection and the water had been drained, she removed the water ramp she used to deflect the stream and then looked at Arlo.

"Would you mind an assist?" She looked up at him with a smile.

"How can I help?"

"A quick burst of dragon fire will turn all of this algae and vegetation to ash, then it would be easier to finish cleaning out."

"Good idea." Arlo smiled. He burned the algae with a good gust of fire and when the smoke had receded, Kyrea reached for a shovel. "What are you doing now?" Arlo asked.

"I'm going to shovel the ashes out."

"Let me help." The dragon turned his back to the fountain and then proceeded to flap his wings. The ashes flew up into the wind and off like a cloud.

Kyrea was thrilled. The fountain looked clean now, so she placed her palms together, rubbed them, while whispering a few words and then opened them, creating a dark cloud growing above the fountain. Within a minute, there was a rumble of thunder and then a gush of rain escaped the cloud directly above the fountain. Kyrea cleaned her hands and legs then went to put her shoes back on as they waited for the fountain to fill up.

Before long, it was full and flowing like a fountain should be. But the water was quite cloudy.

"Why does the water look like that? I thought we did a good job cleaning it out?" Arlo sighed.

"If you let cloudy water settle, it will become clear. If you let your upset mind settle, your course will also become clear."

"Another Monk saying?" Arlo asked. Kyrea nodded. They sat there watching the water flow, Kyrea on a bench, Arlo curled up on the ground next to her. They were both very happy with their work. They sat there peacefully listening to the trickling sound of water flowing until the birds came back to investigate and drink from it. Glancing at each other with smiles, they both felt satisfied.

The sun was starting to set when the garden gate opened. "Oh!" Ms. Mary exclaimed as she walked up to Kyrea who was sleeping on the bench.

Kyrea slowly opened her eyes and stretched, "I'm so sorry, Ms. Mary, I fell asleep. I can leave if you want…"

"It's quite alright dear." The elderly lady smiled as she glanced over at the crystal-clear waters flowing through the fountain. "Did you do this?"

Kyrea smiled, "we felt it would be a nice thing to do…" Kyrea stopped when the sound of the bucket full of coins was knocked over by Arlo's tail. Coins loudly scattered across the path. Still invisible, yet shimmering with his movement, Arlo was slowly skulking away to hide in the bushes.

"Now how did that happen?" Ms. Mary inquired as she looked at the coins on the ground. Kyrea kneeled down to collect them back into the bucket. Mary helped. "Are all of these from the fountain?"

"They are. I collected them hoping to donate them to the orphanage."

"Aren't you sweet?" Mary grinned. "This garden was so popular, for so long. Everyone threw in wishing coins when they came to visit." Mary stopped to look at an odd-shaped coin. It was octagonal with a square hole in the center. A bright green patina had consumed the copper coin but Mary knew it wasn't anything she could spend. "You should take this as a thank you."

"What is it?"

"I don't know. A medallion of sorts I guess."

Kyrea took it into her hand and inspected it closely. She tried to pick at the green patina with her fingernail though it didn't come off.

"Just soak it in some vinegar. It'll come clean. Join me back to the house. I can spare some."

"I'll do that, thank you."

That evening, after they left in search of shelter, flying over to a nearby mountain range in hopes of locating a small, unoccupied cave to spend the night in, the dragon's invisibility wore off.

"Good thing we are almost there." Kyrea spotted and pointed out a cave just up ahead.

"Why is that?" Arlo inquired while changing direction and getting ready to land.

"Because you are no longer invisible."

Arlo spun around to see himself, but the sudden motion caused him to lose his balance. He basically tripped, in mid-air, spiraled into a clumsy somersault, and then tumbled like an uncontrolled cartwheel crashing into the cave with a jarring thud.

Having leaped to safety as he neared the ground, Kyrea ran up to him in utter shock. "Arlo are you alright? What happened?"

He stood up but spoke nothing. He shook out and straightened his wings, stretched his neck and gathered his poise. Kyrea was looking all over the dragon for cuts, scrapes or wounds, he seemed fine.

Finally, he spoke as if he had never crashed at all. "So... the invisibility cloak doesn't last very long... apparently?"

"Three things cannot be long hidden: the sun, the moon, and the truth."

"Is that another monk saying?"

Kyrea nodded her head and smiled.

"CURIOUS ETCHINGS & RUNES…"

Kyrea spoke softly while staring at the medallion.

Arlo pulled from his slumber with a deep inhale and opened his eyes. He saw Kyrea staring at the medallion watching the sunrise through it. Its orangey-pink copper surface gleamed in the sunlight. Its octagonal edges had intricate etchings, but it was the square hole in the middle which caught her attention the most. She was holding it up to the rising sun, taking turns looking through it with her left eye, then her right. Upon closer inspection, she noticed something unusual, a tiny screw thread on one side of the hole, so small it could only be seen under the bright natural light.

"Any ideas what it is?" Arlo stretched out his front legs and neck to release the crick in his muscles.

She squinted, running her finger around the delicate threads. It was a clever design, hidden in plain sight. "Whoever made this put some serious thought into its construction. But what is its purpose? And how did it make it into the fountain?"

"You said there were many tourists who visited the garden, maybe a traveler?"

"Yes. You are right. Especially in this decade. When I first met Mary, she was much younger and air travel was not as common."

"When was that?"

"Oh gosh… it was sometime in the Victorian period. But many decades have passed since then."

Arlo looked at her quizzically, "I'm from medieval times and Mary is from Victorian times, how many years is that?"

"From your era to the Victorian era? Hmmm… somewhere between 500 to 800 years give or take. And from the time I met Mary as a child to now could have been 60 to 70 years? So yeah, a lot could happen in that span of time."

"I jumped ahead in time 800 years?" Arlo looked up trying to grasp how much time that was. "So when you said people hadn't seen dragons in a very long time, what did you mean?"

"You remembered that, did you?" Kyrea cringed at the thought of this conversation.

"Dragons are well-known for their excellent memories." Arlo scowled at her.

"No one has seen a dragon in a long time, it doesn't mean they no longer exist."

"Are dragons extinct?" Arlo about choked.

"You are still here." Kyrea tried to calm him with facts but it didn't seem to help.

"So, if I hadn't gone through the portal, dragons would be extinct?!"

"I don't know, they could be in hiding. You have to remember humans have not populated every place on the planet, nor can most of them travel to different realms. Maybe dragons left medieval times and went to a different realm, a safer world?"

"How will I find them?"

"I don't have all of the answers Arlo, but I have a feeling we will find out. If other dragons exist, we can find them." Kyrea tried to calm him.

"If!" Arlo paced, his wings flapping violently.

"Arlo…"

"He continued pacing in the cave, his tail smacking the rock walls when he turned. She could see he was deep in thought.

"Arlo… are you okay?"

He continued pacing for another minute but then finally stopped, lowered his head and sighed.

"Arlo?"

"I guess I should thank you for saving me."

"You should do no such thing Arlo! You saved yourself. You chose to follow me through the portal. You didn't have to do that. Something told you to take a great leap of faith and you did. Maybe a higher power wanted to save you for a reason.

You know, intuition is not a forgotten sense. It's the ability to understand something without conscious reasoning. You had an instinct or feeling which told you to do this and you listened. It takes a great amount of trust and willpower to take that leap. You are a very special dragon and I am certain you are not the only one who was presented with an opportunity and listened."

"Thank you anyway." Arlo half smiled, knowing what she said was inspiring but still feeling like he was the last dragon on earth.

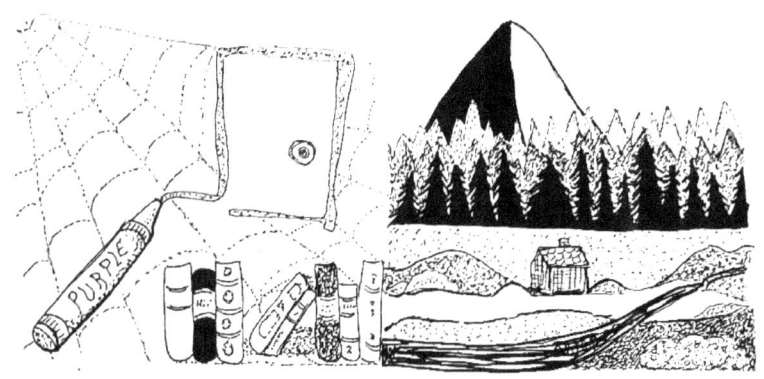

UNLOCKING THE

PAGES OF MAGIC

CHE SUN WAS DIPPING LOW in the sky, casting long shadows across the dense, tangled forest as Kyrea and Arlo made their way down an overgrown path. They had been traveling together for a couple weeks now. Exploring the hidden parts of a world he hardly recognized. The leaves of ancient trees whispered softly in the wind, their branches heavy with vines, and the air smelled sweet, like the promise of rain.

"We're close," Kyrea glanced up at the dragon. Her eyes gleamed with a knowing sparkle. "There's a place I know of, just up ahead. A lovely house where we can stay for a while."

The dragon, with his massive wings folded neatly against his back, rumbled in acknowledgment, his deep golden eyes scanning the winding path ahead. "I hope it's better than the last few places we've stayed. The last one smelled like old apples."

Kyrea chuckled. "This one's different."

The two of them continued walking the narrowing path. The air grew colder as night approached, and soon the only sounds were the soft rustling of leaves under their footsteps.

Finally, they came upon a clearing, where a small house stood at the edge of the trees. But the house was not as she remembered it. The wood was weathered, the roof sagging, and the shutters hung loosely from their hinges. Moss had overtaken much of the structure, covering the once-cheerful cream walls in a blanket of green.

The dragon paused, his nostrils flaring. "Are you sure about this? It looks... well, not at all like I had expected from your description."

Kyrea's smile softened, and she placed a hand on the dragon's massive claw. "I know," she said, her voice tinged with nostalgia. "It's been a long time since I've been here. It's not what it once was, but it still holds grand memories."

She stood silently for a moment as if remembering something long past. Then, with a coy glint in her eyes, she raised her hands. A soft light flickered around her fingers and, with a gentle wave, she cast it toward the house. As the light touched the crumbling structure, the house transformed before the dragon's very eyes.

The walls shimmered with a soft glow, and the roof straightened, returning to its original grandeur. White gingerbread trim outlined the windows like icing on a cake, and colorful peppermint candies adorned each doorframe. Candy cane poles lined the front porch, and the cobblestone path glittered with a dusting of sugar crystals.

The dragon blinked, astonished. "That's... incredible. It's beautiful."

Kyrea smiled. "It was. But time... time has a way of changing things."

They walked up the path together, the dragon marveling at the transformed house. Once inside, the warmth of a crackling fire greeted them. Kyrea lit a candle, and they settled into the cozy living room. The dragon, cold-blooded in nature, sighed contentedly, stretching his wings out slightly as he curled his tail around his feet.

"So, tell me about this house," the dragon said. "Why is it like this now? It doesn't feel like it was always so... forgotten."

Kyrea leaned back, her fingers tracing the rim of her cup thoughtfully. "It wasn't always like this," she began. "But which story should I tell?" she wondered aloud.

"What do you mean *which* story? Isn't there just one story?" Arlo inquired.

Kyrea smirked at him knowingly. "Oh Arlo, if only there WERE just one story, this world would be so much simpler to navigate." Kyrea stood, walked over to an old dusty bookshelf and scanned it for a book. Pulling a small children's picture book through the cobwebs, she blew off the dust and showed him the cover. His eyes opened wide as Kyrea settled down in an armchair and began to read it to him. When she was done, she closed the book and glanced at the dragon who was entranced.

"So that is the story of this house? It belonged to an evil witch?"

"Nope," Kyrea spoke as she slid the book back into the empty spot on the bookshelf. Then she turned to Arlo. "That is the children's version of the story."

"Doesn't seem like much of a children's story, the witch tried to eat them?!?" Arlo scoffed.

"Not children's story like the genre, the actual children from the book told the story. Though… That is not the whole truth."

"So the children lied?"

"No. They didn't lie, they didn't know the whole truth. Do you think a woman like that would decorate her house with gumdrops and candy corns? No way! Adults don't want their house attracting bugs and rodents." Kyrea shook her head.

"So, who did own it?" Arlo perked up curiously, his eyebrows raised.

"This house," Kyrea spoke with a knowing grin, "was actually built by a gnome."

"A gnome? So why was the witch in it? Did the children mistake the gnome for the witch?"

Kyrea chuckled. "Let me explain." She sat back down on the chair and started. "This house was the fulfilled dream of a sweet, young gnome. She left her village to build a beautiful and inviting place of wonder. When she finished, people from all around came to see it. Children loved it. Animals loved it. It was the heart of everything wonderous in the forest."

The dragon nodded, listening intently.

"But when the witch came wandering up and saw the house, looking around, tasting the porch railings, skulking around all scary-like, well, it frightened the gnome. She fled out the back door and went into hiding in the yard."

The dragon's brow furrowed. "How did she hide in the yard? Wouldn't she be seen?"

"Gnomes turn into garden statues."

Arlo furrowed his brows, "Statues?"

"They do, but that is another story." Kyrea quipped. Continuing her thought, she went on. "Do you think the children or the witch saw a lone garden gnome statue standing in the shadows of a nearby tree when the smell of gingerbread and the colorful candy trim caught their eyes? Nope."

Arlo grinned. "Well, I'll be darned."

Kyrea nodded. "It didn't take long for two children, two innocent children, to wander up the path. They knocked on the door, and the witch answered. She warmly invited them in, and then slammed the door shut and locked it."

The dragon's eyes widened. "I'm afraid to ask…. What happened to the children?"

"I just read you the story."

"But you said it was their story, not the truth."

"But all stories are based on truth..." Kyrea sighed deeply, her gaze drifting toward the fire. "They managed to escape, but not without a struggle. The witch was dealt with, and the gnome, heartbroken by what had happened inside of her beloved home, tried to move on. She decided to remove all of the decorations; the candy, the gingerbread trim, everything which gave it life and wonder. But over time, the house lost its joy, and her, with it. Lonely and desolate, she returned to her village, older and somewhat wiser."

"That's horrible," the dragon pouted. "So sad."

Kyrea smiled faintly. "It's a sad story, yes. But it's also a reminder that not all stories are told the way they should be. Today, people only remember the children's version, the one with the witch in the house. No one remembers the gnome who made it beautiful in the first place."

The dragon furrowed his brow. "But why? Why was her story forgotten? Why did no one question the children about the witch's candy-covered house? They never connected the fact that the witch was not the original owner of the house?"

Kyrea looked at the dragon, her eyes filled with understanding. "Because the children wrote the story. And they only told it from their perspective. They didn't know about the gnome's love for her house.

They only knew about the witch and the danger she posed. Sometimes, the real story gets lost."

Arlo huffed as he contemplated this. "She should have written her own storybook." He was deep in thought when Kyrea added another level to his thought process.

"And that is why there will always be more and more books!"

Arlo glanced over at the bookshelf. "Maybe I should write a book someday."

"Maybe you should...." Kyrea smiled, but first, you should spend some time reading all of the stories written about you first."

"Me?" Arlo's eyes sparkled like diamonds.

"Well, about dragons in general."

"Why?"

"To know what stories have been told. You see, when stories are told, they tend to be one-sided. Every once in a while, you might get the other side, but do you know what you don't get? The stories from everyone else."

"What do you mean?" Arlo inquired.

"Like when a bad guy shoots at the good guy running to safety, that flying arrow does tend to hit something. Something which most likely belongs to someone the story isn't even about. But no one talks about that person or how it affected them."

The dragon stared at her for a long moment, considering her words. "You know," he said slowly, "if I had my own story written, it wouldn't be anything like how the knights tell it."

Kyrea raised an eyebrow. "Oh? How's that?"

The dragon huffed, a puff of smoke curling from his nostrils. "They think I'm a beast to be hunted, a monster to be slain. They don't understand dragons. They never will."

Kyrea chuckled softly. "That's true. But the story they tell isn't the only one. There's always more to it. The knights, the people, they only see what they want to see. They don't know the full truth."

"Like the children and the gnome," the dragon said, his voice quiet.

"Exactly," Kyrea replied. "Just because your story hasn't been written yet, doesn't mean it shouldn't be."

The dragon smiled, a gleam of pride in his eyes. "Well, if anyone were to write your story, I suppose it would be... a knight chasing a witch on a metal contraption, with a dragon blocking the path to let her escape."

Kyrea laughed. "That's one way to tell it."

The dragon's smile grew wider. "But they might not understand the connection. The real reason I was there, helping you escape. They might think I was just another monster."

"Maybe," Kyrea said thoughtfully. "But maybe, one day, someone will tell the story as it really was."

The dragon's eyes softened as he looked out at the forest beyond the window, the night deepening around them. "Maybe so. But for now, I'm happy to just be here with you."

Kyrea's smile expressed a gentle understanding. "I'm glad you are too."

And so, as the fire crackled in the hearth, the dragon and Kyrea sat in silence, knowing even if the world didn't remember their true stories, they would always remember each other's.

And perhaps, that was enough.

That night, after Arlo fell asleep, his deep breathing filling the quiet room, Kyrea pulled out the brown leather diary she had acquired. She had been reading for hours, flipping through the pages of the diary. She carefully turned another page, her eyes scanning the princess's elegant handwriting as she read aloud to herself.

"Dear Diary,

The giant returned to the palace today. This time, he didn't just steal the tapestries, tables and chairs; this time he stole our armoire! He ripped the roof off the silo, reached down and snatched the French wardrobe that displayed my family's magical shoes! Without those shoes, we've lost all of our magic abilities! The shoes were enchanted. He got my emerald slippers that granted a healing power, my sapphire stilettos which gave me visions of the future, Dad's diamond Derbies that gave him strength and invincibility and Mom's golden boots, which always dropped a gold coin from the heel with every fifty steps she took."

Kyrea's brow furrowed. The princess's distress was palpable, and she could almost see the royal chambers, a once sparkling display of fine ornate furniture, now haunted by bare walls and empty rooms due to the giant's thievery. She flipped the page and continued reading.

"I sure wish I would have been wearing those diamond shoes before the giant came again, I may have had time to warn the guards. Not that they can do anything against a giant. Perhaps that is why he keeps returning because he knows he can take anything he wants without repercussions. But the big question is, why is he taking everything?"

Kyrea paused, her fingers tracing the edges of the worn pages. It seemed the giant was not only stealing from the palace but also creating a strange little kingdom of his own.

"He started with a small cottage from the shire. Then he returned the next day for a larger cabin. The families of those houses were grateful they hadn't been home, but imagine their shock when they did get home that night only to find their entire home gone, literally lifted up from the ground.

But the thievery continued. The next day was the sheriff's house, a beautiful white, two-story home with more than a dozen rooms. They had just finished building it and had not even moved in yet when the giant absconded with it. The entire town was flabbergasted by the theft but when the giant didn't return for a few days, they started to believe it was over. But it wasn't. He stole the woodworker's furniture first, a couple of beds, and a dining table. Those pieces of furniture had been crafted for townsfolks who had already paid him for his time.

And yet, the next day he returned, this time focusing all of his attention on the castle. Apparently, his tastes were becoming more refined. He stole crystal chandeliers, credenzas full of golden goblets and silver utensils. He stole metal armor and shields, gold inlaid mirrors, the feasting table and chairs, my father's throne and then today, my armoire. It was almost as if he were outfitting his new house with our fancy furniture, but to what end? It was not like HE could live in the house or sit on the throne or wear my emerald shoes. He is a giant. He's way too big!"

Kyrea set the diary down for a moment, thinking. The story was one of desperation. Why would the giant steal from the kingdom? And why would he steal such small things? Surely, he couldn't use any of them, he was much too large.

She glanced out the window to the forest and her eyes caught sight of a rather worn birdhouse. The gnome had decorated it like her house used to be. There was a small porch with gingerbread molding and a door that opened to what was once an adorably decorated birdhouse, complete with wall-to-wall carpeting and wallpaper.

Then it occurred to her. The giant was not stealing for himself, and he was not kind-hearted enough to be creating houses for the giant critters of his world to live in, but he could be decorating a dollhouse for his young daughter…

The next morning Arlo woke with a burst. "I want to write a book!"

"Good for you Arlo, I think that is an excellent thing to do. But don't you think you should read some more books first? You can learn so much about the many centuries you jumped past in our time-traveling adventure and it will help you pass the time." Kyrea spoke as she scoured the pantry for something to eat.

He let out a dramatic sigh, his claws tapping lightly against the stone floor as he glanced toward Kyrea. "But I want to *have* adventures. Not read about them." His scowl was apparent.

Kyrea, her back to him as she filled the pot with water, glanced over her shoulder and smiled. "Why don't you try reading some of those books I've got stacked up over there?"

Arlo raised an eyebrow, skeptical. "We read the one last night, isn't that enough?"

Kyrea chuckled softly and set the spoon down, walking over to him. She crossed her arms, looking at him with a knowing smile. "You never know. You might learn something."

Arlo snorted, shaking his head. "I doubt it."

Kyrea wasn't deterred. She paused for a moment, thoughtful, then quoted a phrase that always stuck with her. "The Taoist monks have this saying: *'We mold clay into a pot, but it is the emptiness inside that makes the vessel useful. We fashion wood for a house, but it is the emptiness inside that makes it livable. We work with the substantial, but the emptiness is what we use."*

Arlo tilted his head, looking at her curiously. "What does that mean?"

Kyrea smiled and gestured toward the pan sitting above the fire on the stove. "Take a look at the pan. What's the most important part of it?"

Arlo stared at the pan for a few moments. "Well, the bottom's the most important, right? It's what protects the food from the heat. It's what collects the heat and warms everything up. So, it's the bottom."

Kyrea shook her head with a soft laugh. "Nope. It's not the bottom."

Arlo frowned, clearly puzzled. "Well, then it's got to be the sides. The sides keep the soup in, so everything doesn't spill out. It's the sides, isn't it?"

Kyrea smiled again, this time a little wider. "Nope. Not the sides either."

Arlo was starting to get frustrated now. "Then it must be the handle. The handle keeps you from burning your hand when you need to move it. The handle's the most important part."

She shook her head again, still smiling. "No, Arlo. You're still wrong."

Arlo gave the pan another thorough inspection, his eyes scanning every part of it carefully. "Okay, I'm stumped. There's the bottom, the sides, and the handle. What else is there?"

Kyrea walked over and placed a gentle hand on his shoulder, guiding his gaze to the empty space inside the pan. "The inside space is the most important part of the pan. It's what matters most."

Arlo looked at her, furrowing his brow in confusion. "The inside? What do you mean?"

Kyrea turned so their eyes met. "It's the space inside the pan that makes it useful. You could have the bottom, the sides, and the handle, but without the inside space, it wouldn't work. It's the space where you put things; the food, the water for tea, whatever you need to warm up, that's what makes the pan valuable."

Arlo blinked a few times, taking in her words. "Okay, I get that. But... how does it answer my question about books?"

Kyrea took a deep breath, then answered with a thoughtful tone. "Books are like the pan, Arlo. Your head, your mind, it's like the empty space. You've got the potential to hold all sorts of things inside you, but unless you fill that space with knowledge and ideas unless you spark the flame of reading and let your imagination run wild, you'll never reach your full potential. Just like the pan without anything inside, your mind won't be truly useful until you fill it with what you learn. Books give you the contents, the stories, and ideas that nourish your mind."

Arlo's eyes lit up as the realization hit him. "So, you're saying I need to fill my head with all sorts of stories, like putting food in the pan, to get the most out of life?"

Kyrea nodded. "Exactly. The stories and knowledge you read are like the ingredients in the pan. They feed your mind. They give you the nutrients you need to think, to imagine, to grow. Without that, you're just an empty vessel, waiting to be filled."

Arlo sat back on his haunches, thinking for a moment. "Okay, that makes sense now." He glanced over at the stack of books Kyrea had mentioned earlier. "Maybe I'll give it a try. It's not like I have anything better to do."

Kyrea gave him a playful wink. "You might be surprised what you find in those books. You never know what you might learn."

Arlo nodded slowly, a grin tugging at the corner of his mouth. "Alright, I'll give it a shot. But no promises on making it my new favorite pastime."

Kyrea laughed, turning back to the soup on the stove. "One step at a time, Arlo. One step at a time."

And with that, Arlo wandered over to the stack of books, picking one up with a curious expression. All of the books were small and skinny and had colored pictures throughout. "Why do these look different than the one you were reading last night?"

"There are all sorts of books. Books for all different age groups, audiences and genres. I thought you would appreciate starting with the children's books as they are the most fun to read."

"Children's books? But I am not a child!"

"You don't have to be a child to read them or appreciate them. Besides, children's books have more historical accuracy than some history books."

Arlo glanced up at her with a disbelieving scowl on his face.

"Don't believe me? History books are written by people who don't believe in magic. They can't wrap their heads around the fantasy world and all of the marvelous things that can happen there. But the people who write children's books have imaginations open to all possibilities. Much of the time, children's books have more facts because they not only blame magic for the occurrences that create the plot, they lean on it."

"Sounds to me like they make it up."

"Every story, even children's books is based on and begins with something real."

Maybe, just maybe, there was something to this after all. Arlo thought to himself. He collected the pile of books and curled up in the corner to read.

After eating Kyrea put on a pair of overalls and gardening gloves.

"What are you going to do today?" Arlo asked glancing up from his book. Two other children's books already in his 'read' pile.

"I was thinking we'd stay here for a while. I have a project I want to work on, a garden actually."

"Like the secret garden behind the wall?" Arlo referenced from earlier.

"I'll be growing something very specific and very large, but first, I have to create the seed. It will take a while to complete. So if you are okay with it, I thought we'd stay out here for a while until our next adventure. This will give you time to read through all of those books on the bookshelf."

"That sounds great! Arlo said happily, then a question came to him. "What will you be growing?" But Kyrea had already grabbed a spade and shovel from the table and was heading out the door.

CULTIVATING A GARDEN INVOLVES

A bit of patience and understanding, Kyrea was explaining to Arlo. Arlo watched her digging in the dirt and planting her seeds, but he was not at all interested in what she was doing. He was way more curious about finishing the book he had started. He was sitting there reading when Kyrea announced she would be heading to town to get supplies.

"What supplies?" Arlo asked glancing up from his book. He wondered if he had missed something she had said earlier and felt a twinge of guilt.

"Food, seeds, maybe a few more books."

"Oh good, I'll see you later." He said as he lowered his nose back to his book.

I think I turned a dragon into a bookworm... Kyrea thought with a short chuckle.

That afternoon, Kyrea returned home with bags of food, plants and seeds. She handed Arlo a stack of books as she turned to the kitchen to begin preparing dinner. She was looking forward to this project with a ton of anticipation.

That night, after the soft crackling of the fire had settled into a quiet hum, Arlo found himself curled up on a rug with a book Kyrea had left lying around; a gardening guide on flowers. His massive claws turned the pages carefully, his tail twitching with interest. The book was full of descriptions, facts, and vibrant illustrations of various plants, but one passage in particular caught his attention.

He froze mid-page, his eyes widening as he read a specific line. He looked up at Kyrea, his gaze intense. Then, without saying a word, he quickly glanced back down at the book before looking back at her, completely entranced.

Kyrea, still working on a project near the fire, noticed his sudden shift. "Something wrong?" she asked, her voice light but curious.

Arlo's voice was full of excitement as he exclaimed, "That's it! Wisteria! Of course!"

Kyrea raised an eyebrow, glancing over to him. "The flower? What about it?"

Arlo, practically vibrating with enthusiasm, read aloud from the book, his voice rising with each word. "Wisteria symbolizes long life, immortality, and wisdom. Wisteria has a fragrant smell that can be described as sweet, and floral. Wisteria flowers have a light, lilac and honeysuckle aroma."

He looked up from the book, a sly grin playing on his face. "I knew it! You smell like honeysuckle and lilacs and something... magical." Arlo stood up from his seat, his large form moving over to where Kyrea was sitting. With a playful gleam in his eye, he inhaled deeply, his nostrils flaring out. "You *are* magical!" He declared boldly.

Kyrea, taken aback by the sudden attention, blushed slightly and smiled shyly. "Magical?" She shrugged. "Long life. Immortality. Wisdom... it does describe me." Her voice was soft, a little playful, but there was a hint of something deeper behind her words. *Did she believe her magical abilities gave her the scent of Wisteria, or was her scent the reason why she was magical?* That wasn't confusing to her at all. *Was it a coincidence? Was the scent a clue to her immortality?*

Arlo grinned, clearly pleased with himself for making the connection. He returned to the book, flipping through the pages with renewed interest, as Kyrea went back to her task. The silence of the room filled their ears with a low hum.

But after a few moments, Kyrea found herself distracted. She paused in her work and unconsciously sniffed her skin. Why couldn't she smell what Arlo had described? She leaned back slightly, trying to catch a hint of honeysuckle or lilac in the air, but it was as if the scent was elusive, just out of reach.

Frowning, she shook her head, unsure of what exactly was going on. Arlo seemed so certain, so confident he had uncovered a piece of the puzzle.

Was it possible she smelled different than other humans?

Kyrea glanced over at Arlo, who was lost in his book, his tail twitching in satisfaction. She couldn't help but smile, a sense of wonder creeping into her thoughts. *I knew I was magical, immortal, but I thought the magic was learned from the monks, not necessarily a part of me. I wonder if whatever it was that saved me and made me immortal, gave me this elusive aroma of Wisteria?*

ℭLOWERS, FRUIT & SPIRALED VINES

crept throughout the garden like a wild explosion of color, shapes and textures.

Kyrea's garden was coming along rapidly. She had planted many rows of a variety of seeds and she already had sprouts coming up. She told Arlo she was growing food, tomatoes, cucumbers, green beans, sunflowers and even apples and grapes. That all made sense to him, they were plants they could eat, but then she had created a garden of other plants, roses, elephant ear bushes, morning glory and bamboo?

She explained how she first had to grow the plants but then Kyrea was doing something oddly different. She called it grafting and it was not the typical gardening technique. She explained that at some point she would cut a healthy stem off of a rose, cut into the stem of the sunflower plant, and join the two plants together with a salve. She would then wrap the two plants with wax to protect them as they bonded together and became a different species of flower that bloomed from the newly grafted stem.

"When the new sun-rose goes to seed, I will take them and plant them into a different section of the garden. The rose's thorns enlarged for the sunflower stalk will provide an ample ladder effect. I'll then repeat the same with the large elephant ear plants as we will need an oversized leaf to rest on."

The newly created plants would produce curiously different flowers that would attract the bees who would pollinate and fertilize them, and eventually, the flowers would produce seeds of an entirely different plant. Kyrea would then take those seeds and splice together an additional plant, creating yet another species of flower.

Arlo had no idea why she needed large leaves to rest on or why she was doing any of this. But the fresh fruits and vegetables for dinner were nice.

She explained how she would do this with several different plants, but eventually, they would all make their way over to the green bean section. The entire process was a curious confusion of complicated gardening techniques to Arlo, but Kyrea seemed to know what she was doing.

"The sunflowers will grow large, hearty stalks which can support our weight. The elephant ears will provide landing pads for us to rest on. The bamboo will ensure everything will grow quickly and the green beans will absorb all of those aspects to create a seed that will grow a stalk so large and so impressive, it will take us out of this world!"

Arlo could sense her excitement, but he didn't think the plant would literally take them out of the world. He thought it was a silly phrase she would say, like out of sight. When he was clearly standing in front of her. Either way, he was glad she enjoyed gardening and he definitely enjoyed reading, but as time progressed, he would begin anticipating an adventure. He may be perfectly capable of settling down and being still in one place for extended periods of time, but now that he was free of the medieval knights, he really did want to explore.

That night Arlo glanced at the stacks of books Kyrea had placed out for him. "I have run out of books to read," Arlo announced.

Kyrea had been poring over a thick, leather-bound book she told him she pulled from a portal earlier and Arlo had been intrigued about it all night. The pages were old, yellowing at the edges, with ink stains here and there which hinted at its long history.

Kyrea glanced up at him and smiled. I can get you some more books. She placed a bookmark to save the spot in her book, then closed it, placing it on the side table. She then raised her hands parallel to each other, her palms clasped together. Slowly, and with a great deal of concentration, she expanded her hands and watched as a small light illuminated from between them. Slowly it grew and widened, looking like a lighted ring that kept growing to about the size of a picture frame. She then reached her hand into the portal and moments later pulled out a new book.

Arlo had been watching intently. When she stuck her hand into the portal, it just disappeared. Most of her arm just above her elbow had disappeared inside of the lighted edge circle hovering before her. When she pulled out the book, the portal closed. "I'll bet you will love reading this one." Kyrea smiled as she held it out to Arlo, for him to take. But he couldn't stop looking at her.

"What did you just do?"

"I opened a portal to the biggest library in the world. I love this place! It has so many books inside…" her voice trailed off as she thought about the wonderous place sha had visited so long ago.

"Can I open portals?" Arlo inquired.

"I studied with the monks for centuries to learn this kind of alchemy. Some may call it magic."

"Can I see the library? Can I go visit it?"

Kyrea stared at him for a few long moments; her lips pursed together as she thought about the answer to his question. The book portals she was able to open were not big enough for her to walk through. They were just big enough to see the other side or maybe reach in with her arm. It would take something much more powerful to create an opening the size that a dragon could walk through. She strummed her fingers on the armrest of the chair. *Not a portal. Not a window... She would need...* "a door!"

Arlo raised an eyebrow wondering what she was thinking about.

"I guess it is time to take you to the library."

Kyrea scoured the cabin's bookshelf, looking at all of the book spines that were there.

"What are you looking for?" Arlo asked another question hoping for an answer. He continued to wait until she placed an index finger on the top of a purple book and tilted it out of place.

"I read that book; it's about Harold..."

"Yes it is." Kyrea smiled as she opened the book while walking to her chair. Arlo was so curious his tail was shifting like a rattle snakes' coil.

PULLING A PURPLE CRAYON

She placed the book down on her lap and opened it, turning to the page with the illustration of the purple crayon. She traced the lines of the drawing with her fingertip, and murmured something under her breath as she did. Arlo watched, intrigued, but still not entirely convinced he understood what she was doing.

She closed her eyes with her hands hovering just above the pages. Concentrating. Then with a sudden, almost imperceptible gesture, Kyrea's fingers reached into the book. Actually, inside of the book! Not touching the pages, but within the pages, as if they were liquid.

Arlo's eyes widened as he saw her fingers sink through the page as though the space itself had become soft and pliable, like the pages of the book were a portal, and her hand was slipping through it.

Slowly, she withdrew her hand, and to Arlo's astonishment, she was holding the purple crayon from inside the book.

Arlo sat up; his mouth slightly agape. "What on earth... how did you...?"

Kyrea grinned, the crayon in between her fingers. "It's all in the text, Arlo. The book isn't just filled with stories or pictures. Every word, and every image holds something more. It's like a map to other worlds, and when you learn how to connect with it, you can pull what you need to right out of the pages."

She handed the crayon to Arlo, who took it with wide eyes. He turned it over in his hand, inspecting it carefully. "So you can just pull anything you want to out of a book?"

"Just about." She leaned back in the chair, "It's a matter of focus and intent," Kyrea explained. "It's like... accessing a different layer of reality, where the written word holds power."

Arlo held the crayon for a moment longer before looking back at Kyrea, still in disbelief. "That's... incredible. So, you're telling me, if I pick up a book, you could just pull out... I don't know, a feast? Or a sword? Or—"

"There are limitations." Kyrea interrupted; her voice filled with conviction. "It has to be something connected to the world within the pages. You can't just summon anything you want to out of thin air. The magic follows the narrative, the essence of the tale. You have to know what is inside the book. You have to have read the story."

Kyrea nodded a playful twinkle in her eye. "It's all about understanding what's inside the pages. The more you read, the more you learn, and the more you can pull from them."

"Was that a pun?" Arlo smirked.

With crayon in hand, Kyrea stood up, walked over to the wall and then turned to look at Arlo. She sized him up with her eyes then turned back to the wall with the crayon. She then drew a rather large door on the wall. Then she knocked on the door and watched it open with a low purple glow.

Arlo watched her walk through and he waited. He had no idea where she went. It had always been a wall. An exterior wall. Arlo looked behind him and saw the window. He opened the sash and stuck his head through, extending his neck to where the opened purple door would have led. There was nothing but the exterior of the house.

When he pulled his head back in, he saw Kyrea walking back into the room. She had with her a stack of books in her hands. They still were not as thick as what she was reading, but they were definitely thicker than the illustrated picture books he had read.

"I think you will enjoy these stories." Kyrea placed the stack inside his paws. His claws curled around that stack to hold it together. She returned to her chair and slid the crayon into her side bag.

He placed them on the rug and sat down. He opened the book on top and flipped through the pages, stopping every few to glance at the pages. "Oh good, there are a few illustrations, but wait, none of them are in color."

"You will discover the more you read, the more the story will come to life in your imagination. You won't need the illustrations to experience the adventure; your imagination will fill in the scenes."

"But I like the pictures in the other books."

"I know. I did too, and still do. But there is so much more to the world of writing than that."

Arlo opened the book and was about to begin reading when curiosity got the better of him. He walked over to the purple outline of the door and reached for the handle. However, it was just a crayon drawing on the wall.

"Knock three times," Kyrea spoke up with a smirk. Arlo did so and suddenly the handle became three-dimensional and he was able to take it within his paws and turn it. With a light purple glow, the door opened and he glanced inside the magical room.

"Where, how... What is this place?"

"This door opens to a library. The very old, rarely frequented Hall of Pages. This library has more books than anyone could read in their entire lifetime." Kyrea stood and walked over to him. She scrunched down just under him and stepped inside the library before him. "If you go down the hall and make a left at the shelf that says CHI. All of these books came from that section. It's a category for children's chapter books. Later on, you could venture down to the right where the shelf says FIC."

"Is this library accessible all of the time?"

"With this door, you can visit it anytime you want to. Just remember to return the books you borrow so others will get to read them too someday."

"Where is this library?"

"You know... I don't remember which city it is located in; I visited it once a very long time ago with one of the monks and just memorized its beauty. As long as I can visualize it, I don't need to know where it is, my portals just open to it."

"So that means it is part of the human world?"

"Oh…" Kyrea paused realizing what he was thinking about. "Yes, this is a human place and if you visit it during the day, you may see a human or two. But you can hide from them behind the shelves if you so choose. They wouldn't bother you."

"A human or two? Why wouldn't hordes of people pack themselves inside this amazing building trying to get their hands on all of those amazing books to read?"

"Oh Arlo… that is a very good question." Kyrea sighed with an exhausted huff. "It baffles my mind trying to figure out why the human world doesn't realize the benefits of libraries and the books they contain. They have access to some of the most incredible wonders of the known universe and those books sit on shelves collecting dust, rarely read. Hardly cherished for the treasures they are. It's truly baffling to me."

SALUTATIONS!

The sun had begun to dip below the horizon, casting long shadows across the cabin. Kyrea had been working outside, carefully grafting the vine that would reach up to the giant world. The air was thick with the earthy scent of the soil and the faint hum of magic, as her hands moved skillfully, weaving the living vine together with precision. The process took time, something she didn't mind, she had plenty of it. She had grown used to working in the quiet, knowing her efforts would eventually bear fruit.

Inside, the dragon was settling into a cozy corner of the living room, a pile of books stacked beside him. His tail curled around his feet as he flipped through the pages of the first book he'd found. He wasn't sure what to expect. He'd never been one to read for long stretches, but the more he read, the more he found himself engrossed in the stories. Books were worlds filled with strange lands, magical creatures, and tales of far-off places. It kept his mind occupied as Kyrea worked.

By the time she returned inside, a handful of chapters later, the dragon was entrenched within the story, his head bent low over the pages.

"Salutations!" the dragon said brightly as Kyrea stepped through the door. His golden eyes twinkled with a mix of amusement and genuine curiosity as he lifted his head to greet her.

"What chapter are you on now?" she asked, her voice deep and warm.

Arlo raised an eyebrow, a smile tugging at the corners of his lips. "Chapter five, I think."

Kyrea motioned toward the pile of read books beside him. "You've been busy."

"I have!" the dragon replied enthusiastically, his eyes gleaming. "I've never realized how much there is in books. It's quite... fascinating."

Kyrea gave him an approving nod before heading toward another room, muttering something under her breath. When she returned, she was holding a small, square box in her hands. The dragon eyed it curiously as she set it down on the table beside him.

"What's this?" his brow furrowing slightly.

Kyrea's eyes twinkling with knowledge. She reached into the box and pulled out a few tissues, one at a time, unfolding them carefully. The dragon stared at the soft, white material in her hand with confusion clearly written across his face. "These are tissues, for wiping tears and blowing your nose."

"Tissues?" he asked, his deep voice puzzled.

Kyrea grinned, her gaze bouncing between him and the book he had been reading. "Well, you see," she said, her tone playful, "sometimes when a reader, like yourself, gets caught up in an emotional moment... like, say, a particularly touching scene in a book..." She trailed off, watching him closely. "You might need something to wipe away a tear or two."

The dragon blinked, momentarily stunned. "Tears?" he echoed, looking down at the book in his claws. "I don't... I don't cry."

Kyrea's grin widened. "I think you just might."

"Preposterous!" He scoffed.

"Go on, keep reading. But you'll probably need the tissues towards the end. Just saying."

With a hesitant glance at her, the dragon turned his attention back to the book. As time passed, Kyrea settled down into her own book. The room became eerily quiet as the two of them read.

Finally, with the turn of a page, Arlo's eyes narrowed in concentration. Then, without warning, the dragon's chest seemed to tighten, and his eyes glistened, for just a moment.

His golden gaze glimmered up to Kyrea, who was watching him intently, a knowing smile on her face. "Are you... are you telling me I need a tissue?" he asked, his voice sounding uncertain.

Kyrea just nodded with a slight chuckle. "Go ahead. Don't fight it."

"I... I... I'll just stop reading." He declared with a huff, slamming the book shut.

"Do you really WANT to stop reading?" Kyrea asked carefully.

Arlo glanced at her and then back at the book. How could ink on paper make him feel this way?

The dragon blinked a few more times, his mind struggling to understand the strange sensation in his chest. He hadn't expected the story to hit him like this. Something about this particular moment had gotten to him. It was like it was magic.

Reluctantly, he reached for the tissues and dabbed gently at his eyes, letting out a small, disgruntled huff. "I didn't expect this," he muttered.

Kyrea's smile softened as she settled beside him. "Sometimes, the right story can make you feel things you didn't expect. It's the magic of reading."

The dragon shook his head, still trying to make sense of it all. "I never knew books could be so... so powerful. It's like they... they can change you."

"They can," Kyrea said, her voice warm with understanding. "That's the beauty of stories. They open up your heart, even if you didn't realize it needed opening."

For a moment, they both sat in quiet contemplation, the fire crackling softly in the hearth. Then with a deep breath, the dragon opened the book back up to where he had stopped and continued to read, the tissues now tucked neatly by his side.

Kyrea could see he was absorbing the experience, his mind stretching to understand this new layer of the world. And for once, it wasn't just about the magic inside of the stories, it was about the way those stories could change you, magically.

ᚲᴏ Pʟᴀɴᴛ ᴀ Sᴇᴇᴅ

Oᴠᴇʀ ᴛʜᴇ ɴᴇxᴛ ᴄᴏᴜᴘʟᴇ ᴏꜰ ᴍᴏɴᴛʜꜱ, Kyrea worked tirelessly on her garden project. Arlo, the dragon, watched curiously but couldn't quite grasp what she was up to. He often hung out in the forest, content with his own thoughts as Kyrea busied herself with her peculiar gardening task.

"Once planted," she explained to Arlo one evening, "this final plant should grow quickly. Once it finishes flowering and goes to seed, I will have what we have been waiting for."

"Another seed?"

"A very special seed. A bean seed that will grow faster than any vine you've ever seen. And it will be much bigger, than you could ever imagine. We'll soon have our way into the Giant World."

Arlo raised an eyebrow, his golden eyes full of uncertainty. "Giant World? I don't know if I like that. I'm already afraid of people your size."

Kyrea chuckled. "Oh, the giants are mostly kind-hearted. They grow the most beautiful gardens. When we're there, you'll feel like a little dragon again. You'll be the size you were when you were a child. To them the size of a lizard. You'll be able to enjoy the beauty of your surroundings and soar through the treetops and eat the fruit without a worry or a care in the world.

Arlo's face brightened at the idea. "That sounds like a wonderful place."

Kyrea's lips curled into a smile but her eyes did not reflect the same enthusiasm. While she had never heard of other giants having anger issues, the king of the castle she was planning on visiting, well, he did. And all she could hope for, was that she wouldn't attract his attention while she was there.

THE HALL OF PAGES

The next day, early afternoon, Arlo closed the last book on his to be read pile and placed it with the rest. When he reached for a new book, he noticed he was out. A feeling of disappointment swept over him and he just sat there staring at his pile of read books, wondering if he wanted to read one of them again. He didn't, he determined. He glanced up and looked over at the purple crayon lines on the wall.

He stood and walked to it, wringing his paws together nervously. The library would have more books, an infinite number of books... but this doorway opened to the human world.

What if a human saw him? Would they run away screaming or would they attack him? Would they go in search of backup to overwhelm him? What if he got trapped? What if the door shut and he couldn't get back? His heart was beating rapidly in his chest. He turned away from the door.

When he did, he eyed his pile of books. Oh right, I need to return those. He gathered the pile in his arms and turned back to the door. "I'm a dragon! I can hold my own against those pesky little humans."

With three light knocks, the door handle emerged and he opened the door. The purple glow slowly faded to show an enormous gently lit room.

It seemed as if time itself had forgotten about this library's existence. Dusty beams of light filtered through tall, arched, stained-glass windows, casting long, colorful shadows over the room. Rows of towering shelves stretched higher than any common man could reach, extending far past where his eyes could see. The air smelled of parchment, ink, and a hint of something older, something magical. Thousands upon thousands of books, sat on endless shelves and as the dragon walked further into the library something else caught his attention.

Scrolls and fragile tomes lay scattered across a counter in a separate room, closed off to the public with large black bars creating a gate. Some books were wrapped in leather, others in golden threads, while a few were nothing more than delicate, yellowed scrolls that unfurled like whispers of forgotten stories. This place must have been quite unique as he could tell mere mortals wouldn't be allowed near such historical artifacts.

The dragon slithered silently between the shelves. Though his body was massive he glided through the aisles with grace. His golden eyes glimmered with the thrill of being here. His tail swayed behind him like a giant serpent, swishing past dusty volumes. But as careful as he was, he couldn't hide the occasional rustle of his wings behind him or the soft *scrape* of his tail against the floor.

A strange sense of excitement filled the dragon's chest. These books... oh, these books! Stories from lands he hadn't seen. Secrets of magic long forgotten. Long-lost knowledge, written in the tongues of races long extinct. He couldn't resist. He *needed* these books. But there was one small, nagging problem: what about the humans?

Kyrea said the library was rarely visited, but in the short time he had been here, a few curious travelers wandered in, seeking knowledge. And as much as the dragon enjoyed reading, he had no desire to be seen by them.

Just as he tucked another prized book under his arm, a noise echoed down the hallway. Footsteps. Human footsteps. And they were getting louder... closer. The dragon froze. His heart raced. His breath held in the smoky depths of his chest. There was no time to think; the only option was to hide.

Quick as lightning, he slithered behind one of the stacks of books then leapt on top of the shelf like a cat. Crouched down low, body flattened, but his tail—*oh no*—didn't quite make it over the shelf.

Just keep breathing, he told himself, as he reeled his tail in like a rope. He waited. He watched. He held his tail up to his side with his pile of books he'd collected just under his chest.

The footsteps grew closer. They paused.

Suddenly, a human appeared. A young scholar with a dust-covered cloak and wide eyes behind a pair of thick glasses, scanned the bookshelf. He paused, a book clutched in one hand, the finger of his free hand sliding against the spines of the books on the middle shelf. Then he stopped, tipped a book to the side and placed the book he had been holding in the empty spot. He then walked away.

He hadn't even seen the dragon hiding up there, staring down at him with his nose mere inches away from his head. Arlo released a breath he had been unaware he had been holding.

I could have bitten his head off... if I was hungry.

The dragon exhaled in relief, his massive body sagging against the top of the shelf, his tail dangling just above the floor.

That was close.

After a long pause, the dragon exhaled a sigh of relief. As he turned to the right, he saw the door at the end of the long hallway.

No use climbing down and navigating the stacks, he thought, I'll just leapfrog over the top of these shelves and escape to safety.

As he leaped through the opening of the door, stack of books in his hands, he couldn't help but smile. He had ventured out on his own and it all went surprisingly smooth. Maybe being a part of the human world would work out afterall?

CASTLE

OF THE

SKY GARDEN

ᎢHREE DAYS LATER, Kyrea's special plant went to flower. Two days after, it dropped its seeds. Kyrea collected them and placed all of them in a jar, shy one, then cut down the plant so it wouldn't keep growing. Arlo was shocked.

"Why did you do that?"

"This world does not need a plant that will give them unlimited magical seeds to the Giant World."

"I imagine not." Arlo agreed. "Then what are you going to do with the jar of seeds you saved?

"You see that book over there?" Kyrea pointed to the side table. It was the same very large, old book she had been reading from for the past couple of weeks. Arlo looked at it closely. The weathered leatherbound book reinforced with brass corners had tattered cloth parchment pages as thin as silk. Arlo had looked at it many times over the past week noting it didn't even have a title written or embossed on the cover or spine.

"It's called the Codex of Verdant Vaults. It lists every plant known to man and beyond. In fact, it claims there is a place unknown to any living being where a vault of seeds exists to populate any planet in the universe."

"That is absolutely fascinating." Arlo concurred but was still confused.

"I'm going to store the seeds in the vault. No one without my magical abilities will ever be able to retrieve them, nor would they even know they exist there. They will be safe forever."

"Okay then." Arlo smiled.

The next morning, they found the magical vine had grown quite a bit, stretching high towards the clouds. Arlo was really ready for an adventure. "Can we go to the Giant World today?"

Kyrea looked up at the towering stalk, her eyes thoughtful. "Not today. But I'll water it."

Arlo looked at the stalk, then back at Kyrea, clearly intrigued. "Let's fly up and see what it looks like from above."

Kyrea smiled. "Sure, let's go!" Kyrea rode on Arlo's back as they flew high into the sky, circling the thick bean stalk. As they reached the cloud level,

Kyrea pointed, "See? It's not touching the clouds yet. It's not tall enough."

Arlo circled the stalk, flying closer to see it more clearly. "But it's still growing?"

Kyrea nodded.

"Why can't I just keep flying upwards? Wouldn't I reach the giant world eventually?"

"Not without the magic of the stalk. We can't reach the Giant World until we climb the stalk. The clouds will part as we ascend."

"I don't understand," Arlo soared past the stalk.

"It's all about perspective," she answered. "From where we are hovering now, looking down at this vine, everything looks small, right?"

"That's correct. Arlo flew around the vine to get another look at the world below.

"From up here you can still see our little house we've been staying in. And while it *does* look smaller from way up here, it has not gotten so small that we cannot see it at all. To get to the giant world, we have to go so far, the house will be gone. And that's how we know that we will have gotten there. Because our world will no longer be visible."

"I still don't understand why we can't just fly there today?"

"You could definitely fly up higher, and you will keep flying up higher and higher and higher, but we will never make it to the giant world, because it is the plant that opens the door. It is the plant that leads to the cloud. Let me show you, fly that direction." She pointed up. "As you get closer to the cloud it seems to open up or dissolve." It was like it wasn't really there. They flew into it and they felt the cool moisture, but there was no place for them to land. He touched it with his claws but didn't feel anything solid. "There's no way we can stand on this cloud and not fall down to the ground."

Arlo looked forward to seeing what a cloud that they could land on felt like but he would have to wait.

So, they flew back down to the ground and Arlo watched Kyrea water the stalk. Then they went on with their day.

The next morning, Arlo woke to find that the beanstalk had quadrupled in size. Its girth was as large as the house they were living in, and when Arlo looked up, he saw it go into a cloud so far away that he just knew it led to the giant world.

Arlo couldn't wait to explore! So, while Kyrea slept, he flew up to investigate.

But as he ascended higher and higher, something strange happened; the air grew thin, and he struggled to fly any further. Despite his powerful wings, the air was too light for him to find enough current to keep going. He'd fly up as high as he could, but then he'd descend downwards like a weight. He'd catch himself with the wind and try again, only to be stopped by the lack of air.

Frustrated, Arlo returned to the ground, where Kyrea was just stepping out of the house. "I think today is the day." She smiled as she stretched.

"I tried flying up to the top," he explained, "but the air is too thin. I couldn't get to the Giant World."

Kyrea smiled. "That's why we climb. The stalk will give us the path. It will create its own oxygen for us to breathe, the large grafted plants will support us along the way and the fruit roots will provide food to eat along our long, tall journey. But you'll need to be patient. It will take time. Probably even a couple of days' worth of climbing."

"A couple of days?" Arlo groaned.

After a hearty breakfast, they began their climb. The climb started out easy, especially with the rose thorns to use as ladder rungs, but the higher they went, the more difficult the climb became.

With every step, the world below became a distant memory. Eventually, the clouds disappeared entirely, and Arlo could only see endless white skies above and below them.

They stopped on a large leaf for lunch, and Kyrea pulling a few bunches of grapes from the vine.

Later they stopped for dinner, eating apples and cucumber salad. The moisture in the air collected on the spiraling vines and collected on curved leaves for them to drink from and the rose petals made for wonderful pillows to sleep on.

Before falling asleep, Kyrea took one of the curly vines and wrapped it around her chest.

"Why are you doing that," Arlo asked.

"I'm afraid I may roll off the leaf while I'm sleeping. It's not like I have wings to fly like you do."

"But you're immortal. You wouldn't die." Arlo winked at her.

"Of course... but I'd have to start this journey all over again tomorrow."

"Oh, right!"

By the next night they were so far up they couldn't see anything of the world below and nothing of a world to come. Arlo was beginning to wonder if they would ever get there.

"Of course we will," Kyrea smiled. "In fact, the beanstalk is continuing to grow, so who knows, we may wake up there in the morning."

"That would be awesome!" Arlo began hoping they wouldn't have to climb any more tomorrow.

The next morning as Arlo opened his eyes. He had expected to see nothing but white sky and clouds, but instead, he saw a garden. A beautiful fluffy soft colorful garden. The Giant World had arrived. The landscape was unlike anything he'd ever seen: flowers the size of small houses, trees with leaves that looked like massive pillows, and clouds that had solidified into a soft, trampoline-like surface beneath their feet.

Arlo gazed around at the magnificent world he found himself in, feeling a mix of awe and wonder. The landscape stretched out before him like a dream, with vibrant colors everywhere. The flowers looked soft, almost like feathery plush pillows in every shade imaginable, and the trees, with their wide, rounded trunks, resembled enormous soft cushions. The grass, too, was no ordinary grass. The long blades looked like strands of silky fur, each one soft and inviting. The purple sky above them seemed too surreal to be real, like a sky painted in pastels, blending from lavender to a deeper violet the higher it stretched.

Taking a deep breath, Kyrea smiled as she took in the otherworldly beauty of the giant world. She glanced over at Arlo, who was clearly just as mesmerized by it all. He stood proudly on the soft, buoyant cloud, his paws sinking just a little into its fluffy surface as he tested it. His scales shimmered as the purple sky reflected off of them, and the way the soft white cloud cushioned his every step made it look like he was dancing.

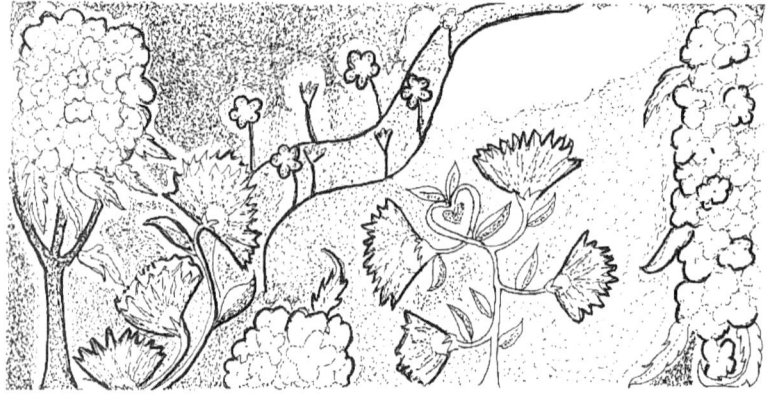

Kyrea made her way closer to him, feeling a slight thrill at how small she was in this vast land. The air was fresh, almost crisp, with the scent of moisture. A cool, clean, earthy smell that reminded her of the moment just before rain starts to fall. It had that clean, refreshing quality, like the world was newly born. She couldn't quite find the right word for it, but it felt both peaceful and invigorating, like a fresh start to a brand-new life.

As Arlo jumped and landed, the cloud responded with a slight bounce, which made him chuckle. It was such a strange sensation, one that made him feel almost weightless, but not in danger. The cloud didn't seem to want to let him fall. His movements were playful, almost childlike, as he jumped again and again, testing the limits of this soft, cloud-like ground.

Kyrea watched him, amused, and couldn't help but laugh softly. "Careful, Arlo," she teased. "You might just bounce away."

He paused for a moment, his eyes wide with excitement. "I don't think I'd mind that," he said with a grin, his large wings unfurling slightly as if testing the air, wondering how far he could go.

Kyrea looked around and spotted a blackberry bush. Of course, up here, the blackberries were the size of Arlo. Each little berry ball (drupelet) was the size of a watermelon. She picked one, rolled it to the side and then sat down, her legs tucked under her.

"I'm glad it's soft," she said, looking at the ground beneath her. She had expected to find solid ground, like dirt, but instead, she was surrounded by clouds that felt like the softest Egyptian cotton.

Arlo, sat down beside her, and let out a low, contented sigh. "I didn't expect it to be so different."

Kyrea smiled, "The world is full of surprises. Let's enjoy this moment while we can." She leaned back, stretching out her legs on the fluffy grass, and gazed up at the sky, feeling a sense of peace. She felt very content, and she was grateful for this moment of peace before her journey.

"Let's eat some breakfast," she said, pointing at the giant blackberry. Arlo was quick to follow her lead, his large paws gently pulling apart the soft fruit with a satisfied grunt.

The soft sounds of their peaceful morning were only interrupted by the occasional rustle of the fluffy grass beside them and the distant calls of unseen creatures in the far reaches of the garden. The garden was full of color and life, yet somehow felt tranquil.

After a peaceful breakfast, Kyrea knew they had more to explore, more to discover in this incredible, giant world. She looked up at the vine in the distance, still towering above them, knowing that this was only the beginning of their adventure.

She also realized anyone could see the stalk and that may have been problematic for the giant world as well as the human world. The last thing she wanted to do was leave magical realms open for others to get through.

Using the same alchemy as she had to make Arlo invisible before, she transformed the vine into what looked like shimmering glass. It just disappeared against the backdrop of this colorful new world.

"What if we need to find it again?" Arlo asked looking at the cloaked plant.

"The spell doesn't last long, as you well know. Since the plant doesn't really move it will last longer than yours did, but it will eventually become visible again." With a deep breath, she stood up, ready to continue their journey. "Shall we?" she asked Arlo, her eyes sparkling with excitement.

The dragon nodded eagerly, his wings fluttering in anticipation. "Let's see what else this amazing world has to offer."

As they made their way down the milky path of frosting-like gravel, the world just grew larger and more marvelous. The sounds of distant creatures were getting closer and so was the Giant's castle that Kyrea was heading towards.

"You know Arlo, we may be here for a while."

"What's a while?" Arlo asked inquisitively.

"I have something I need to do in that castle. It could easily take me a few days to just get there."

"I can fly you over there."

"I appreciate that, Arlo, I do, but you don't need to do that. We are in a fantastic new world. Look at all of this beauty? You should explore it. You should enjoy it. You should go into it and just have fun."

"But what about you?"

"Like I said, I have something to do in that castle. It may take me a week or more just to navigate through it all. And.... It could be dangerous for me, and I don't want to put you in danger as well."

"How dangerous?" Arlo looked concerned.

"I'll be as small as a mouse to the Giant. He likely won't even see me, but being small still comes with its challenges. I am not worried – I am immortal. But you are not. You deserve to let go, enjoy your time in a world where you don't have to be afraid in. No one is hunting you here. You get to be you and you don't have to hold back or hide. Experience that freedom for yourself. Okay?"

"Okay but…"

"If you really want to go with me, I would, of course, love the company, and would absolutely never push you away. But this is something I can do alone. Meet some other species of this world and enjoy yourself. You deserve to have fun."

"Really? You don't mind?"

"Not at all."

"Oh good! Because the last thing I wanted to do is go into that scary looking giant human castle."

"I understand completely. Kyrea placed a hand on his paw and smiled.

$\mathcal{A}$S $\mathcal{A}$RLO WANDERED DEEPER into the lush garden, he marveled at the strange creatures he encountered. The air felt alive with the buzz of enormous insects. It was a far cry from the more familiar landscapes he was used to. Here, everything was larger than life, from the massive trees which swayed above him, to the plants that brushed against his sides. Even the very atmosphere seemed to hum with a strange, magical power.

Then, out of the corner of his eye, something fluttered past him. A butterfly, brilliant in color, fluttered lazily by, its wings a mix of deep purples, vibrant oranges, and electric blues. It was as large as Arlo himself, with wings that shimmered in the sunlight like iridescent jewels. The creature's delicate body seemed to pulse with life, a thing of beauty and grace in this fantastical realm.

Arlo stood frozen for a moment; his mouth slightly open in awe. In the other world, butterflies were so small, barely more than a speck in the air. But here, in the giant world, everything was larger, more intense, more vibrant. The details were massive. The textures amazing.

It wasn't just the butterfly that caught his attention. Everywhere Arlo looked, he saw creatures that were far larger than any he had encountered before. Massive beetles the size of boulders, towering ants carrying enormous leaves that could cover the entire length of his tail, and even birds which soared overhead like living ships, their wingspans larger than the length of an entire tree.

Suddenly, Arlo noticed a rustling in the underbrush. He turned his head, his keen eyes scanning the area for any sign of movement. Then, through the thick foliage, emerged a creature that took his breath away. It was a giant lizard, with iridescent scales that glowed in shades of green and gold. The creature's eyes, large and round, locked onto Arlo's, studying him with curiosity. Its long, neck extended forward, and a strange red balloon-like structure began to expand from beneath its throat, inflating slowly like some bizarre throat sac.

The lizard didn't approach, but it didn't retreat either. It seemed content to observe, its large eyes studying Arlo with a level of intelligence that made Arlo feel like he was being sized up, not as a threat, but as an enigma. Arlo, for his part, couldn't help but feel a sense of wonder as he looked at the giant creature. It was the same size as him, an enormous, majestic lizard with scales that shimmered like liquid metal. He had never seen anything like it before, and he couldn't help but feel both awe and fascination bubbling up inside him.

As he stood there, the lizard continued to eye him, its neck extending again, its throat sac inflating further as it took a slow, deliberate step toward him. But just as quickly, it stopped, as if it had decided that Arlo wasn't worth the risk of further investigation. The lizard blinked slowly, as though considering its next move, before turning and scurrying away.

Arlo watched the creature disappear into the garden, captivated by what he had just witnessed. This world was strange and yet everything was so beautiful. Despite his usual hesitation to get too close to unfamiliar creatures, Arlo couldn't help but feel drawn to the mysteries of this place.

He heard the soft, rapid buzz of wings again and looked up just in time to see a giant dragonfly darting past him. It flitted about with ease, its translucent wings catching the sunlight as it hovered just out of reach. The dragonfly was like no creature Arlo had ever seen. Its body was slender and elongated, and its wings clear with intricate veins running through them that looked like crystal-stained glass. Arlo swished his tail in excitement, watching the dragonfly hover and dart with movements as precise as lightning.

Despite his awe, Arlo couldn't help but feel a bit like an intruder in this strange, enchanted world. He was used to flying high and feeling powerful, but here, he was just one of many regular sized bugs in the sprawling garden of the giant world.

He glanced back at the iridescent lizard, which was now nowhere to be seen, and then returned his attention to the dragonfly, which was slowly moving farther away. As he watched it disappear into the distance, he spotted something else watching him from afar. This one did not slink off. It strummed a musical melody with its back legs and then made a leap so great, it flew over Arlo's head like a rainbow and disappeared into the brush.

That was a grasshopper, he realized, as his jaw just hung open.

KYREA'S HEART BEAT WILDLY as she approached the looming castle gates, the massive stone walls towering over her. The scale of everything in the giant world was overwhelming. It made her feel like a mere speck of dust, a passing flea beneath the monstrous structure. Each step forward felt heavy, even as her feet kept sinking into the soft, pillowy grass that cushioned her movements. Yet nothing could quell the growing knot in her stomach.

She tried to shake off the unease, tried to convince herself that this was what she had set out to do. This was her goal; the reason she had climbed the towering beanstalk in the first place. But now that she was here, standing at the entrance of a castle that seemed to stretch endlessly into the sky, the task ahead felt far more daunting than she had anticipated.

Her eyes darted around, trying to focus on something, anything that might ground her. The birds massive, pterodactyl-like creatures which swooped overhead. Their wings beating with such force that the wind from their flight sent ripples across the soft land beneath her. They didn't seem to notice her, or perhaps, they simply didn't care. Everything here was too large, too strange, too... foreign.

Kyrea wasn't used to feeling small. She had always been the one with the magic, the one with the power to create and command, but standing before this castle, she was no more than an ant compared to the giants who might reside within. It wasn't the fear of the unknown that gnawed at her, but the sheer scale of it all. What if she didn't find what she was looking for? What if the dollhouse she had traveled so far to find, was no longer here or never was? What if the giants had abandoned it long ago, or worse, destroyed it in their monstrous whims?

And then there was Arlo.

Her mind jumped to him, the dragon who was now lost somewhere in this huge world. He had set off to explore, his excitement apparent as he bounded through the garden with carefree abandon. But she couldn't help worrying about him venturing out alone. Arlo was brave and strong, but this world was unlike anything either of them had ever known. Strange creatures, towering trees, and the ever-present threat of the giant.

What if something happened to him?

It wasn't that she doubted Arlo's ability to handle himself. Far from it. But just because he was a dragon didn't mean he was invincible. What if Arlo stumbled into trouble? What if he didn't make it back to her? What if she couldn't find him when she was ready to go? What if he didn't want to leave when she did find him?

What a sad thought! I truly love his company!

Shaking her head, Kyrea quickly pushed the thought aside. She had a task to focus on. A castle to explore. A dollhouse to find. Arlo would be fine. He was strong. He could handle whatever came his way. She had to believe that. But as she glanced back over her shoulder, her heart felt tight, like there was a heavy weight pressing against her chest.

With a deep breath, she turned toward the massive gates once more. She couldn't afford to waste time on worry. She had come this far. She had a goal. The dollhouse wasn't going to find itself.

Yet, as she stepped closer, her nerves tightened again. Was this truly a good idea? What was she walking into? Would the giant's wrath come crashing down on her for even daring to enter his domain?

With every step, Kyrea felt smaller, the castle more oppressive. Her heart pounded in her chest as she reached the giant wooden door. Her fingers brushed the surface of the cold, weathered wood, and she hesitated for another moment before squeezing through a crack like a mouse entering a barn.

ARLO COULDN'T BELIEVE HIS EYES as he stood there, the enormity of the world stretching out before him. Everything was so much bigger. Towering trees with leaves the size of sailboats, flowers with petals as large as blankets, and basic looking bugs that dwarfed him in size. But the most incredible thing of all was the group of lizards sliding down the giant leaf, shrieking with joy as they soared into the air, flipped a couple of times and then dove gracefully into a shimmering lake below.

He couldn't help but smile at their carefree laughter. The sight of them made him feel a little braver, a little more at ease in this overwhelming world. He stepped closer, his heart pounding with a mix of excitement and nervousness, and as he did, one of the lizards noticed him.

"Want to join us?" the lizard called out, a big grin on his face.

Arlo blinked, surprised, then grinned back and nodded enthusiastically. He had no idea what they were doing, but it looked and sounded like the most fun he'd had in ages. "Sure!"

The lizard swam over to the shore and climbed out of the water. "New here?" he asked, his eyes sparkling with curiosity.

"Yeah," Arlo replied, his voice a mix of awe and excitement. "I just got here. This place is amazing."

"What's your name?" The lizard puffed up, excited to show Arlo the ropes.

"Arlo."

"Hi Arlo! Come on, let's have some fun!"

Arlo hesitated for a moment, watching the other lizards climb the tree to get to the slide-looking thick blade of grass. He watched them zoom down the leaf slide one by one, their laughter filling the air. They'd reach the curve up at the end and fly up into the air, pulling off a twirl or spin or flip then dive gracefully into the waters below.

They seemed to be having the time of their lives, and he wanted in. His adrenaline was spiking, but it felt like the good kind of scary, like he was about to do something thrilling.

He stepped up to the top of the leaf, looking down at the others who were now waiting for him in the water. They were cheering him on, calling his name with enthusiasm.

"Arlo! Arlo! Arlo!"

The chant filled him with a rush of courage. He was still nervous, but the energy of the group made it easier to ignore his fears. He took a deep breath, scooted his tail to the edge, and pushed off.

For a moment, the world around him blurred as gravity yanked him down the slide. He picked up speed, faster and faster, the wind whipping past his face. His heart raced and lifted to his throat as he neared the bottom of the slide, where the leaf's tip turned upward, launching him into the air. For a brief moment, he felt weightless, suspended in the sky like a feather caught in the wind.

But then reality hit.

His stomach dropped, and a sense of panic bubbled up inside him. He wasn't flying; he was falling! The fear crept in. What if he hit the water wrong? What if he belly-flopped or splashed in awkwardly? Worse, what if he couldn't swim? He had never tried swimming. *Why was that?* He wondered quickly then realized – *my dragon fire!*

His wings snapped open instinctively, and with a sudden rush of air, they caught the wind. He wasn't falling anymore. He was soaring. The panic melted away, replaced by a soaring sense of freedom as he glided safely passed the water. He landed softly on the shore, his heart still racing but now filled with exhilaration having done something so wild.

The lizards, who had been floating in the water, stared up at him in awe. Their eyes were wide, their mouths agape. Silence stretched between them, and then, all at once, they erupted into cheers.

"Wow! That's so cool!" one of them shouted.

"You can fly!" another gasped.

"You were holding out on us!" someone else laughed and walked up to him.

Arlo's cheeks flushed with pride, but he didn't have time to savor the moment before more lizards were clamoring around him with excitement.

"Can you take us flying?" they asked in unison.

Arlo grinned. He had never been asked that before, but the thought of giving them the thrill of flying was too irresistible to pass up. He flapped his wings and took to the sky again, this time, swooping down to scoop up one of the lizards in his claws.

The lizard clung to him, laughing, as Arlo soared higher and higher. Then, as they neared the lake, he released the lizard, letting him fall freely toward the water. The lizard screamed with joy as he plummeted and then splashed down. Arlo followed with another lizard, creating a chain of joyful friends that soared and dove in delight. The laughter was contagious, echoing through the air as he flew them like a roller coaster, up, down, and around in the sky.

When he finally landed back on the ground, the lizards were practically bouncing with excitement, their eyes gleaming with admiration. "Arlo, you're the coolest lizard we've ever met!"

Of course I am, Arlo thought, *I'm a dragon.*

That night, Arlo stayed with the lizards, enjoying their company and their hospitality. They invited him to dinner, a feast of oversized fruits and strange delicacies from the garden, all served in dishes too big for him to imagine back in his normal world. The night was filled with laughter, stories, and more flying. He had forgotten just how strange the world around him had been when he first arrived.

For the first time since entering the giant world, Arlo felt like he truly belonged. And, perhaps more importantly, he realized he had just made a whole new group of friends.

Kyrea's journey into the Giant's castle seemingly had only begun. The wooden doors she slipped through were actually only the gates of the kingdom. She still had to make it across the town, to the moat and bridge, then across the bridge and into the castle. *Were her feet hurting? No. It was just in her imagination.*

She spent many hours scurrying across open lands, keeping to the shadows of nearby buildings and then treading across thick grassy knolls. It had been a long journey, but she was getting closer.

As she neared the moat and drawbridge, she heard a curious sound, a soft honking that echoed like a mysterious song. Intrigued, she followed the noise and found a massive goose gliding gracefully in the castle's wide moat.

The goose, enormous enough to make Kyrea feel super small, turned its head toward her as she approached, its eyes fixated on her. Despite the bird's imposing size, Kyrea wasn't afraid. She was determined to find what she had come for.

"Hello, there!" Kyrea called, standing on the stone edge of the moat. "I'm looking for something in the castle. A dollhouse maybe. Do you happen to know where it might be?"

The goose tilted its head; its long neck stretched elegantly toward Kyrea. "Ah, little one, I know the castle well, but I've never seen such a thing as a dollhouse." *Of course*, it thought to itself, *I don't know what a dollhouse is… but I'm sure I haven't seen one.*

Kyrea's heart sank, but she wasn't about to give up. "You know the castle well?"

"I am a special goose, much beloved by the Giant, so I can wander anywhere in this grand place."

"Hmm… Do you know which wing in the castle I could start searching? Or any room a child may hang out in?"

The goose ruffled its feathers. "I can't say, but I do know this: If you're looking to visit the castle, I could take you there myself. I am about to head back inside. You're small enough to ride on my back, and I'd be happy to give you a tour."

Kyrea's eyes sparkled. "Really? You'd do that for me?" She fawned over the goose's generosity.

"Of course," the goose replied with a quizzical honk. "It's no trouble at all. And perhaps we'll find your dollhouse along the way."

With a grateful smile, Kyrea nodded. "I'd love that. Thank you very much."

Without hesitation, the great goose dipped its head low, allowing Kyrea to climb onto its back, her legs barely straddled either side of the bird.

With a graceful push, they glided forward. The goose gently paddled through the moat, its wings making rhythmic splashes in the cool water that flowed beneath the castle's walls.

As the goose navigated the waterways beneath the castle Kyrea marveled at the coolness of the air and the echoing sounds of distant footsteps. Her heart thudded with excitement as they passed under the very foundations of the Giant's home.

They swam up through narrow passages that twisted through the castle and emerged in the cool, shadowy basement. The air was damp and smelled faintly of the ground before rain. Due to their small stature, they were able to slip between the bars of heavy iron doors, and made their way up a dark set of stairs. Arriving in the sprawling dungeon, Kyrea saw chains and forgotten relics hung on the walls.

"I don't think I'll find a dollhouse down here," Kyrea mused with a shiver of foreboding.

"No?" The goose replied, its voice soft. "But we're on our way to the kitchen now. There's always something cooking there."

The air grew warmer as they entered the kitchen, the rich smell of roasted meats and fresh-baked bread wafting around them. Kyrea's stomach growled, but only because it smelled so good.

The goose's feathers puffed out in pride. "The Giant's cook is renowned for making feasts fit for kings... and giants."

They continued through the grand hallways, each room more extravagant than the last. Rich tapestries adorned the walls, depicting ancient battles and mythical creatures, while gigantic metal suits of armor stood guard at every turn. The air was thick with the scent of old wood and cold stone. The halls echoed with the soft rustle of the goose's wings as it glided smoothly past.

"This room," the goose said, slowing down as they passed a grand chamber with a high, vaulted ceiling, "is the Giant's throne room."

"Oh my! Is he in there?"

"I don't know. Would you like me to go see?"

"No!" Kyrea's heart skipped a beat. She definitely did not want to meet the giant. Changing the subject she asked, "is there a library?"

"There is." The goose smiled brightly. "He loves to read about distant lands and forgotten magic. But I don't think you'll find a dollhouse there."

Kyrea laughed lightly. "Worth a shot. And if no dollhouse, there is most certainly a map of the castle I can take a gander at. No pun intended." She giggled.

"I wouldn't know." The goose admitted shyly, "I don't know how to read."

They passed dozens of rooms, each more magnificent than the last, but Kyrea's eyes were always searching, scanning for any sign of the tiny home she sought.

Finally, the goose stopped in front of a towering set of double doors, intricately carved with ancient symbols. "And here," the goose said, "is the library."

Kyrea's curiosity was piqued. She slid down the gooses' wing and then smiled. "I'll check inside. Thank you so much for the tour. It's been amazing."

The goose gave her a warm, beak-shaking nod. "Don't mention it. I'm glad to help."

Kyrea, paused before turning towards the library, "I'm curious, have you ever heard of anything that could grant wishes or do magic?"

The goose shook its head no. "Haven't heard of anything like that. But the library might have information about it."

"I have every intention on looking that up while I'm here," Kyrea admitted. She turned to the door but the goose spoke again.

"Beware, little one. The Giant doesn't take kindly to uninvited guests poking around his home. There was this boy once..."

Kyrea grinned. "Don't worry, I'll be careful."

As she approached the doors, she couldn't help but feel a spark of excitement. She had the whole castle before her, and with the goose's help, she was a giant step closer to finding what she sought.

Kyrea squeezed through the narrow crack between the massive doors of the library and stepped inside. She had to take a moment to let her eyes adjust to the dim light and the overwhelming scale of the space. The library was massive; not just because the books themselves were large enough for a giant to hold, but because there were so many of them. Books on bookshelves stretched to the ceiling. The shelves seemed to go on forever, a maze of towering bookcases filled with not only books, but all sorts of odd knick-knacks. Strange, glittering objects and curiosities caught her attention.

As Kyrea wandered deeper into the aisles, her small feet barely making a sound on the thick, dust-covered floor, she couldn't help but be amazed at the sheer amount of things to explore. She had a mission, of course, but part of her just wanted to stand still and drink it all in.

Her eyes scanned the giant's disorganized piles of books, trying to make sense of the chaos, her head tilted backward as she gazed at everything before her. When suddenly, *thud*, she tripped over something warm and soft. A small gasp of shock escaped her lips as she looked up to find herself face-to-paw with a massive cat. It was sprawled out across the floor, seemingly asleep.

The cat slowly opened one eye. His gaze shifted down to the small girl standing right in front of him, and Kyrea's breath caught. While she didn't look like a mouse, with the big round ears and long thin tail, she was definitely the size of one.

The cat raised his head, staring at her for a long moment. He stood with surprising grace for such a large creature, towering over her like a lion. He slowly stretched, letting out a low, rumbling growl from deep within his chest.

Kyrea had no doubt that sound would send the bravest of knights running for cover, but she stood her ground, somehow unshaken. "Hi, I'm Kyrea," she said sweetly, patting the large, soft paw closest to her.

The cat's eyes narrowed as if in disbelief. His paw jerked away from her touch, only to return to its resting position. Kyrea noticed the way he favored the other, almost as if it was bothering him.

"Are you okay? Is something wrong with your paw?" she asked, her curiosity outweighing her fear.

"I'm fine!" the cat growled, but as he stepped forward, his paw twisted slightly, and he winced.

"You *are* hurt!" Kyrea said, reaching out despite the cat's growls. "Let me see it."

"No," he hissed yanking his paw away from her.

"Come on, I won't hurt you. Let me help," Kyrea's voice soothing, even though her heart raced.

After a moment of tense silence, the cat seemed to relent. He carefully lay down on his belly, turning his paw up to reveal a thorn lodged between his thick, padded toes. Kyrea bent closer and noticed the thorn and skin around it had been aggravated by the cat's constant licking, in hopes of pulling it out.

With a deep breath, Kyrea reached for the thorn, placing both hands around it, and with a firm tug, she pulled. The cat yelped, springing back in surprise and pain, but when he put his paw down again, he flexed it, testing it carefully. The pain was gone.

"You got it!" The cat said with a mix of surprise and gratitude. "Thank you."

"You're welcome, Mr. Kitty," Kyrea grinned.

"Fluffers," the cat corrected, his ears flicking in irritation. "Fluffers. My name is Fluffers."

Kyrea raised an eyebrow, trying not to laugh. "Fluffers, huh? That's a good name. It's very... descriptive." She gestured to his thick, luxurious coat of fur. "Definitely *fluffy*."

Fluffers gave her a lopsided look. "You *do* have a way with words, don't you, little one?"

"Kyrea," she replied while pointing to herself, smiling warmly. "It's nice to meet you, Fluffers."

After the basic introductions were out of the way, Kyrea explained her purpose; "Do you know where I might find any books on magical creatures or magical artifacts? Maybe something on wish granting?"

Fluffers stretched, clearly feeling better after the thorn removal. "Books? I know where those are. I can help you!" He jumped to his feet, his large body moving gracefully as he climbed up one of the towering shelves with ease, his paws swiping through the rows of books. With a mighty swipe, he knocked a book loose from the shelf and sent it tumbling down toward Kyrea. Dodging as it landed with a heavy thud, she bent over to read the spine and realized this was not the book she needed.

"See if you can find any with weird symbols on them, or mention crystals, or wizards..." Kyrea kept rattling off possible themes. While she did the cat bounded from bookshelf to bookshelf, pawing at books and yanking them off the shelves with his claws.

"Oh, and see if you can find any that mention faeries." She added. There was another project she needed to research.

The cat bounded across the bookshelves, glancing at book titles, and then with a smirk, knocked another book off of the shelf.

She opened it, flipping through the pages as quickly as she could. But the books were huge, each page like a giant rug she had to drag, inch by inch, across the floor. It was exhausting work. She'd pull the corner of one page, tread across it, and the next, and then drop the page, only to turn and pull the next corner over until the page was flipped.

Fluffers was relentless in his help, knocking down book after book for her to work through, while Kyrea read every single word she could, determined to find something specific.

Hours passed, then the sun began to set. Kyrea, tired and bleary-eyed, glanced up at the clock. Time had slipped away unnoticed. She had lost track. The entire day had slipped into night.

Yawning, she found a comfortable spot near Fluffers' soft, thick fur. Without even thinking, she curled up and fell asleep right beside him. His fur made an excellent blanket, warm and fluffy, and before she knew it, she was out like a light.

LIZARDS AFTER DARK

It was late afternoon when the lizards finally emerged from the cool water to dry off and soak up the warmth of the setting sun. Their scaled bodies glistened in the fuchsia light as their long tails swished lazily in the breeze. A chorus of low chatter filled the air as they exchanged stories and laughter. The sounds of distant birds singing their evening songs, serenaded the group. Something that sounded like large crickets fiddling a tune was like a musical concert of joy.

Arlo sat among them, his long wings folded neatly behind him, so he could blend in better with the vibrant community of lizards. A few of them were lounging, while others gathered nearby, discussing the day's events. It felt nice, a stark contrast to the world he left before he met Kyrea.

I wonder how she's doing, he thought.

One of the lizards, a particularly colorful one with fiery orange scales, turned to him and asked, "Where are you staying tonight, Arlo?"

Arlo blinked, a little caught off guard. He hadn't given much thought to where he'd be spending the night. "I don't know, actually. I just got here this morning," he admitted, scratching his head. As a dragon, he could sleep anywhere, but his answer felt strange; being in a new place with no plan.

The lizard smiled kindly. "Then you will stay with us." Arlo couldn't help but feel reassured by the warm invitation. As he nodded his head, she introduced herself. "I am Lizzy."

"Arloculotomous. But my friends call me Arlo."

"Arlo is a wonderful name." she smiled.

That evening, as twilight deepened and the stars began to prick the dark purple sky, everyone pitched in to prepare a simple but hearty meal. The scent of roasting vegetables and fresh herbs wafted in the air. The crackle of the campfire as it blazed brightly, casted long shadows around the clearing. Laughter rang through the night as the group shared stories, some humorous, others hauntingly beautiful.

The lizards made him feel welcome. He listened intently, soaking in the vibrant history of this world, though it all felt so foreign. It was almost like a dream, this peaceful gathering beneath the sky.

As the firelight began to wane, casting the camp in deeper shadows, Arlo stood up to stretch his legs. He decided a walk might help clear his head.

He followed a narrow path that wound through thick trees. The air was crisp, and the night sky above sparkled with a million stars. Yet those stars looked so close they seemed to pulse with a strange, rhythmic energy, as though they were breathing. It was mesmerizing, but also disorienting to Arlo. He had never seen the stars so close up before.

Suddenly, a rustling sound broke his trance, sending a shiver down his spine. From the shadows, a figure emerged, a lizard, but not like any he had met today. Its scales were a dark gray, almost translucent in the dim light, and his eyes gleamed with an unsettling sharpness. Something about his presence made Arlo's pulse quicken, his instincts screaming at him to be cautious.

The lizard approached slowly, deliberately, eyeing Arlo with an intensity that made him uncomfortable. "You're the one who can fly, aren't you?" the lizard said, voice smooth like oil. "I've never seen a lizard like you."

Arlo, instinctively opening his wings a little wider, and was about to correct him and say he was a dragon, but something stopped him. The words hung on his tongue, and he chose to remain silent, unsure of the lizard's intentions.

The strange lizard circled Arlo, pacing around him like a predator sizing up its prey. Arlo felt self-conscious; every movement of the lizard's eyes made him more uneasy. His skin crawled as he instinctively took a half-step back, his gaze darting back toward the campfire.

"You are the coolest lizard I've ever met," the strange lizard continued with a grin that seemed more like a snarl. "I'd like to introduce you to my friends."

Arlo felt a chill creep up his spine. Something about the way the lizard spoke, the way it circled him, the way his eyes blinked twice, didn't sit right. His gut told him this was no friendly offer. The thought of returning to the warmth and safety of the campfire suddenly seemed like the wisest decision. He glanced toward the group, still visible in the distance, and spoke firmly. "I think I'll return to the group. You're welcome to bring your friends there if you like."

The lizard's grin widened, but the smile didn't reach his eyes. It was a hollow thing, sharp-edged, and it made the proverbial hairs on the back of Arlo's neck stand on end. "That's cool. Maybe we'll get together tomorrow," the lizard said, its voice dripping with something unspoken.

"Okay then," Arlo replied quickly, taking a step backward, then turned toward the path that led back to the fire. But as he walked away, a sudden thought struck him, and he turned back toward the lizard. "What's your name?"

The lizard, still grinning, stood in the shadows, the darkness swallowing him up in a way that didn't make sense. In the blink of an eye, he was gone, vanished, as though he had never existed. No rustling of leaves, no crunch of dirt beneath his feet. The night air was silent and Arlo was again, alone.

Arlo stood frozen for a moment, staring into the empty space where the lizard had been, his heart pounding in his chest. A cold shiver ran down his spine. Whatever that lizard was, he wasn't just strange, he may have been dangerous.

Kyrea woke up early the next morning. The sun hadn't even contemplated peeking over the horizon and Kyrea was already back at it, reading. As the midday sun broke through the threshold of the west-facing library window, Fluffers began to stir. He sat up, licked the sleep from his face by wetting his paws and wiping, and then stretched when he felt suitably clean. He then padded off to find food or whatever cats his size did during the day. As he approached the library door, he pawed at it until it creaked open enough for him to slip through.

That'll be helpful later, Kyrea thought to herself.

Kyrea reached into her side pouch and pulled out some berries to munch on. She had saved them from the day before, knowing she'd need sustenance for her voyage.

Then she returned to her reading. There was so much to learn, so much to explore in these large dusty books full of forgotten lore. She put as much knowledge as she could into her memory, knowing well the human brain is capable of retaining much more than the average person thinks it can.

Evening was near when Kyrea finally closed the last book. She sat down on the spine with a sigh of exhaustion and then looked up to the walls. That's when her eyes were drawn to a framed map hanging on the far wall of the library. The map was yellowed with age, the ink faded, and the paper curling and disintegrating on the edges. But as Kyrea inspected it closer, her eyes noted new writing on it, writing that didn't match the rest. It said nursery, and suddenly it all made sense. Suddenly her original reason for visiting had been confirmed. The giant *did* have a daughter. Now she was certain the reason for all the thieving from the townspeople. If the child wanted a dollhouse, the giant would stop at nothing to fulfill that wish. She was now certain this is what she came here to find.

She inspected the map closer, discovered her location, the library., and then continued to scan how to get to the nursery. It was marked near the castle's highest tower a good trek away from where she was currently. A normal trek for a giant, an epic journey for someone the size of a mouse.

Suddenly exhaustion took over. Not only had she been reading all day, and she realized she needed to eat again, the realization of the trek ahead of her mentally wiped her out. She yawned, feeling her eyes grow heavy. Tomorrow. I'll begin my journey to the nursery tomorrow.

As morning ascended upon the castle, Kyrea made her way out of the library and gazed down the hallway. The shadows seemed to lengthen, stretching ominously across the stone floors and towering walls. Even an immortal like Kyrea couldn't help but feel the cold grip of fear crawl up her spine. The enormity of the place, the long corridors and the suffocating silence of the castle, made her feel smaller than ever.

She inhaled deeply, closing her eyes to ready herself, when a darkness approached, blocking the light shimmering before her closed eyelids. When she opened her eyes she saw fur, and lots of it.

"Fluffers." She chuckled looking up at the cat. "You startled me."

"Are you leaving?" He looked sad.

"I am. It's time for me to head to the nursery." She paused, thinking, and then hesitated before speaking again. "Fluffers, I hate to ask, but is there any way you could help me get to the nursery?" Her voice low with a hint of trepidation as she pointed to the map inside of the library.

Fluffers, who had been contentedly sitting in front of her, glanced up at the map. He squinted at it, cocking his head, clearly not realizing it was a map. After a moment, he gave a single, decisive nod, as though the whole thing made perfect sense.

Kyrea raised an eyebrow. *Was the cat actually playing smart, or was he just going along with whatever?* "The giant's daughter's room?" she clarified, narrowing her eyes.

"Oh yes, I know where it is," Fluffers purred, his whiskers twitching. "I can get you there, but not inside. I'm not allowed inside the little girl's room."

Kyrea sighed grateful. "To the door will be great. It'll save me quite a long walk."

With that, Fluffers leaned forward, allowing Kyrea to climb onto his back. Then he slinked ahead, leading the way down a dark, labyrinth of halls. After some time, they reached a heavy wooden door that stood before them like an imposing fortress. Fluffers stopped and laid down. "This is it."

Kyrea leaped from his back to the floor and then he stood quickly. With a nervous angst to his voice he spoke, "Good luck." Then he sped down the hallway as fast as a bolt of lightning.

Without a word, Kyrea approached the door and studied it carefully. The metal handle was so high, it might as well have been in the clouds. She knelt down, peering beneath the threshold, but there was no room to squeeze through.

Her mind raced. If this was a new door, then the giant parents must have been trying to keep things out, like mice, or critters as small as me.

As her gaze shifted upwards, she noticed the gleam of a keyhole, its size just right. *If I can just climb up to the handle, I should be able to get in.*

But how?

A glance around revealed nothing useful, until her eyes landed on a spider in the corner, weaving a delicate web. The perfect solution, it seemed. She approached it cautiously.

"Excuse me," Kyrea's voice soft but tinged with urgency. "I was wondering if you could help me?"

The spider, startled at first, paused in its work and blinked with its multiple eyes. Kyrea quickly explained her predicament, detailing her need to climb the door to reach the handle. The spider tilted its head, sizing her up.

"I can't carry you. You are much too big," the spider said in a matter-of-fact tone.

"I wasn't asking for that," Kyrea confirmed. "I was thinking you could crawl up there and tie a string to the handle, so I can climb it."

The spider raised an eyebrow. "What string?"

Kyrea's gaze swept around the room, landing on a worn, tattered tapestry hanging on the wall. She pulled at one of the loose threads until it came free, unraveling a long, thin line. Within moments, she had created a rope just long enough to reach the handle. She bit off the end of it, tying a secure knot. "Can you do that?" she asked, holding the rope out.

The spider eyed the rope, considering. "Sure, I can. But what's in it for me?"

Kyrea paused for a moment, *I guess I am asking for a big favor...* then remembered something. "I saw a trail of ants just down the hall. Someone dropped a chunk of bread and it attracted them. I can show you where it is."

The spider's eyes gleamed at the mention of food. "I *am* hungry..."

"Deal?" Kyrea asked.

The spider nodded quickly and scuttled up the door, its tiny legs moving with lightning speed. It reached the top in no time, and soon the rope was secured to the handle. The spider spun a thin layer of web around it, ensuring it would stay firm, and then lowered the rope down to Kyrea.

Tugging on it to check its security, she then began to climb. Though this was a lot more difficult than climbing a beanstalk, the rope held firm.

Halfway up, she met the spider again, this time coming down. "The ants?" The spider's legs twitched with excitement. "

Kyrea smiled and nodded. "Down the hall, to the second passage way, third door to the left."

The spider skittered off eagerly, leaving Kyrea to finish her climb, alone.

Finally, she reached the door handle, its massive size looming over her. She sat there for a moment, legs dangling over the edge, feeling the exhaustion from her climb begin to settle in. "Whew," she muttered under her breath.

From up here she could see a lot more of the castle, well the hall of the castle, but she didn't feel quite so small as she had when she was on the floor. It went a long way to set her at ease.

Once she gathered her energy, Kyrea stood and turned to the keyhole. She could fit, just barely.

Peering through, she could see a faintly illuminated room beyond, the soft glow of sunlight shining through a curtained window. In the center of the room sat the object of her quest, the dollhouse, perched like a treasure chest, undoubtedly full of riches.

Kyrea took a deep breath and pulled the rope through the keyhole, letting it fall to the floor on the other side. Then, with a swift motion, she slid down the rope, landing lightly on the floor of the nursery. The room was just as large and ominous as the rest of the castle, but the dollhouse gleamed invitingly. Plus, she could see it was open on one side. She wondered how the giant ripped the back off the sheriff's house, to make this more like a dollhouse, but that was neither here nor there. As she neared, she began eyeing the bed on the second floor. Her exhaustion weighed on her like an anchor. She hadn't slept much the past couple of days... maybe a short nap would do her good?

Kyrea climbed the stairs to the bedroom. She crawled beneath the covers and sighed as the soft fabric enveloped her. For the first time in what felt like forever, she allowed herself to relax.

She then drifted into a deep, peaceful slumber.

HANG GLIDING LIZARDS

The next morning, Arlo woke up in a strange new world. While this had become a somewhat common occurrence for him lately, today something felt different. The air around him was thick with the smell of rain and the distant scent of sweet berries. As his amber eyes opened to the greatness of the giant's world, the sky greeted him with a soft, pearly pink. The dew droplets the size of Arlo's head, shimmered on the towering plants like a blanket of sparkling jewels.

He stretched his wings brushing against the soft grass, sending dew flying into the air like scattered stars. With a gentle grunt, Arlo stood up, his claws sinking slightly into the marshmallow-like ground. He looked out across the small clearing where he noticed his new lizard friends. They were busy gathering ingredients for breakfast.

What struck him most was how well they worked together, their little reptilian hands exchanging fruits and nuts to create a feast for all. It was a welcome change from the isolation he had known most of his life.

Arlo watched them for a moment longer, his heart swelling with warmth. The sense of camaraderie among the lizards was contagious, and he found himself eager to be a part of their day.

As the group settled down for breakfast, everyone began discussing what to do today. Would they explore new parts of the world, or continue their adventures in the familiar territory around them?

"Maybe we should give Arlo the grand tour of the giant world," suggested a young lizard with sparkling purple eyes, his tail twitching in excitement. "The trees are so huge, and the berries are ripe for the picking! Or we could climb the tallest tree!" He grinned widely, his sharp teeth glinting in the morning light.

"Or ride the river!" another lizard added.

Before Arlo could offer his thoughts, a raspy voice emerged from behind a cluster of flowers.

"Maybe Arlo can take us for a flight," that creepy lizard from last night hummed. Its eyes narrowed with mischievous intent. The chameleon stepped into view, giving a wink towards Arlo which made him raise an eyebrow of curiosity.

"Oh, I would love to fly again!" a younger lizard squealed, her voice high-pitched with delight.

"Me too!" another chimed in, tail wagging.

Arlo smiled but then heard the voice of a female lizard, her tone gentle but protective. She walked over to Arlo. She placed a hand on his shoulder, looking up at him with concern.

"That sounds exhausting for Arlo, he's our guest. We shouldn't be putting him to work," her voice was warm yet firm.

The others hesitated, their excitement waning slightly as they considered her words.

"But... maybe he can just fly us over to the garden," the creepy lizard suggested. "I'll bet the strawberries are ripe."

At the mention of strawberries, several of the lizards' eyes practically glazed over in longing, their tongues flicking out in excitement.

"You know we can't go there," the female lizard reminded them, her voice steady. "If the giants find us, we'd be nothing but green puddles of smush."

"Maybe he can teach us to fly," suggested one of the other lizards. Everyone turned their attention to the lizard up on the stem of a tall flower, then upon themselves. *That was a great idea,* they murmured amongst themselves.

Arlo thought for a moment, the idea swirling in his mind. "I'm not sure I can teach you," he said thoughtfully, "you need wings to fly." With that, he spread his wings wide, their enormity casting a shadow over the group.

One of the younger lizards gasped in awe. "That is so cool! I wish we had wings."

One of the other lizards had been watching the group from above, hanging onto a large floral stem as he stood on a rather large leaf. He looked down at the leaf and thought it looked a lot like Arlo's wings. "Can we use these big leaves as wings?"

The crowd of lizards gasped with wonder and excitement. "What a brilliant idea!"

"Well," Arlo said, scratching his head, "the leaves here are big enough to be wings, but how would you flap them?"

One of the lizards, who had been darting about, climbed up a flower stem and crawled under a large leaf. "Our arms!" he said with a wide grin. "We can flap our arms, like this!" He wiggled his arms in the air, mimicking the movement of flying like a bird.

"Yeah," another one joined in, "We just need to figure out how to hold onto the leaves." He scratched his chin thoughtfully.

Arlo's mind raced, his imagination running wild. He had read stories about humans trying such feats and failing. He had seen pictures of humans with wings on their arms, humans in balloons, and humans creating gliders long before the first airplane…. That's when a spark of inspiration flashed within him. "All you need is to turn a large leaf into a giant wing, like a hang glider," he said, his voice quickening with excitement. "It has to generate lift to counteract gravity. If you run, or catch the wind, you'll soar!"

He paused for a moment, the gears in his mind clicking together. "Bring me a couple of those big leaves, some sticks, and vines. I'll make you a glider."

The lizards scrambled to gather the materials, chattering eagerly. The female lizard walked up to Arlo, "you don't need to do this if you don't want to."

"It's fine. It'll be fun. I just read about these contraptions, so I think I can build one."

"My names, Katrin," she said as she stuck out her hand. "It is a pleasure to meet you."

Within twenty minutes, Arlo had crafted a makeshift glider, tying the leaves securely with vines and fashioning a control pole for them to hold onto. He was explaining the dynamics of flying as he built it. "To generate lift which counteracts the gravity you will have to run and catch the wind. Or maybe carry it up a nearby hill and then run off the edge."

Everyone was discussing the possibilities when Arlo tied the last knot. "Okay, try it out!" Arlo called to the nearest lizard.

The others watched in breathless anticipation as the young lizard ran up the nearby hill, the glider held tightly in his hands. He hesitated for only a moment and, with a nervous but determined leap, launched himself into the air. The wind caught the leaf wing, lifting him up like a kite caught in a storm. His body soared briefly before crashing into the soft earth below with a gentle thud.

"It didn't stay up in the air," the young lizard groaned, getting up and dusting himself off. "But that was so much fun!"

"You have to run, or take it up higher and jump off a cliff!" Arlo suggested with a grin. "Catch the wind, like a bird!"

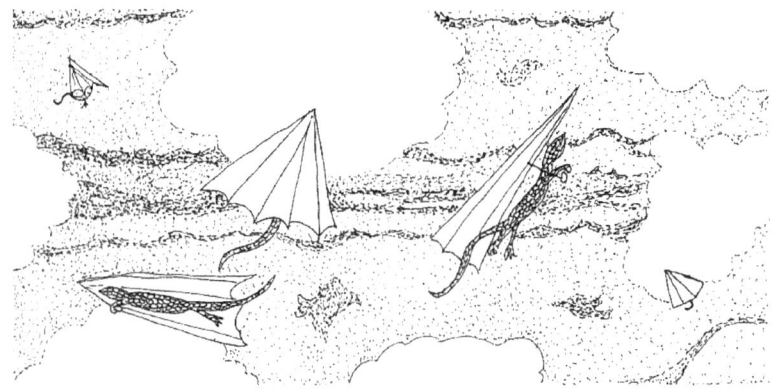

By mid-afternoon, Arlo had crafted nearly a dozen hang gliders, each one a little more refined than the last. The lizards were ecstatic, laughing and cheering as they glided—well, almost glided—down the rolling hills. To Arlo, it looked more like controlled falling than true flight, but to the lizards, it was nothing short of magical.

One by one, they launched themselves into the air. Their excited squeals rising as they learned how to harness the wind. Their hearts were soaring as high as their bodies. Arlo watched them with a deep sense of satisfaction. A proud smile spreading across his face. Today, in this strange new world, he had given his friends the gift of flight, something, perhaps, they would never forget.

The next morning when she awoke, Kyrea was temporarily mystified by her surroundings. As she stretched and yawned, the details began to come into focus. The room was beautiful, fit for a princess. Pink satin sheets, a comforter so soft it could have been made from chinchilla fur.

Above her, the four-post bed stretched toward the ceiling, its golden netting shimmering like spun sunlight. The red velvet curtains, thick and heavy, surrounded windows so clear it was as if there was not any glass.

But when she glanced out the windows, instead of the expected view of sunshine, trees, or chirping birds, she found a child's room, with shelves of toys, a wardrobe full of clothes and an enormous bed intricate carvings on the four-poster frame.

"Oh right, I'm in the Giants castle." Kyrea chuckled as she stretched, then rose from the bed.

But there was no time to get lost in awe. *Today*, she had work to do. Her task was clear. She had to find the shoes from the princess's diary.

The problem was this dollhouse was no mere toy. It was the size of a mansion. The day before, she'd only managed a cursory glance at the opened side of the house. She hadn't had the time or the energy to properly explore, but from what she could see, there were dozens of rooms, and each of them had to be searched thoroughly.

Her gaze scanned the room, trying to work out where to begin. Every wardrobe, every chest, every dresser seemed like it could hold the answer.

"Alright, first things first," Kyrea muttered to herself, feeling a surge of determination. "I can do this. I've made it this far."

But deep down, she knew it wasn't going to be easy. If she didn't move quickly, the giant's daughter may spot her. The thought made her heart race with a bit of nervousness. The giant's daughter may be a small child, but she could still squarsh Kyrea in her hands without trying. She could still step on her if she weren't looking, and though Kyrea wouldn't die, she was fairly certain she would get hurt.

With a final glance around the room, she slipped out of the bed and landed lightly on the soft carpet, her small feet barely making a sound. Today, she would find what she came for.

Starting in this room; she checked every piece of furniture. The chest of drawers, the hope chest, the wardrobe, and the vanity. She even looked under the bed though she was certain she wouldn't find the shoes there. She did find the princess's makeup and silver hairbrush in the vanity, and quite a few gorgeous gowns in the wardrobe. Kyrea had half a mind to try on some of these beautiful gowns as she hadn't been this close to clothes these gorgeous in eons. Sliding her hands down the soft, shimmering fabric, she lifted the long lace arms to her cheek.

Why couldn't I have been a princess? She wondered as she let the sleeve slip from her fingers.

Because I wouldn't be immortal, and be able to have these grand adventures, she scolded herself.

Clothes, toiletries, but no shoes. Why wouldn't the princess keep her shoes with her dresses?

Unscrupulous Chameleons

While the lizards were joyfully experimenting with their new hang gliders; leaping from towering heights, seeking even greater summits, soaring through the air, crashing with gleeful abandon, and learning the art of landing; Arlo decided to take a walk. This world was nothing short of mesmerizing. It was so colorful, so soft, so inviting, yet it made him feel startlingly small. Every blade of grass seemed like a towering monument to nature's grandeur, and the nearby trees loomed like colossal mountains. It wasn't just the scale that made him feel tiny, it was also the fact that his new friends were all absorbed in their own adventures. And maybe, just maybe, it was because he found himself missing Kyrea.

How was she doing?

He wandered aimlessly, lost in thought, until a curious scent stopped him in his tracks, a sweet, earthy fragrance that beckoned him to explore. A flower stood nearby, soft and round, its pink poofs feathering out in delicate wisps. The stem seemed to hold dozens of these "triple-decker lollipop-like blooms." The scent was an enchanting blend of lavender and ripe plum. *Mmmmm....*

He leaned in closer to inhale its fragrance of the strange bloom. As he pulled back to admire the entire plant, a glimmer of movement caught his eye. Suddenly, there was a lizard. A chameleon, shifting in hue as the light filtered through the air. He had blended seamlessly with its surroundings until it stirred. *Had he been standing there the whole time?*

"Hello again," the lizard greeted him with a familiar voice which was startlingly calm.

Arlo blinked, taking in the sight of the chameleon. Its dark, almost shadowy skin shimmered with hidden shades, becoming a riot of color as the sunlight danced across it. Despite its strange appearance, the lizard no longer unnerved him as much as it had in the dark of night.

"Hi again," Arlo responded, tilting his head in curiosity. "Were you standing there the whole time?"

The lizard chuckled. "The name's Eleon," it said, extending a hand that shimmered in the light. "You've made quite the impression on the garden, you know. The lizards are off having a grand time with that flying contraption you made them."

Arlo smiled, feeling a little pride swell inside him. "Oh, would you like one too?" he offered, still amused by the lizards zipping through the sky.

Eleon's eyes gleamed. "I thought we'd hang out together, see what we can learn from each other."

Arlo considered this. He wasn't sure why, but there was something about Eleon's presence that made him feel warry. With a shrug, he agreed, though he still felt a twinge of hesitation. The two began walking together, their conversation meandering from lighthearted small talk to more curious and probing questions.

"Yeah, in the real world, there is this book about..." Arlo began but was interrupted.

"The real world?" Eleon laughed, the sound echoing lightly in the breeze. "What does it make this place, then?"

"The *giant* world," Arlo replied, but as soon as the words left his mouth, he wondered if he should have said it. He hadn't actually asked what this world was called, and admitting that everything here was giant could become a problem if they ever left it.

Eleon led him down a winding trail to the left, though Arlo had intended to go right. He didn't mind following the lizard's lead, after all, Eleon knew this world better than he did. The path soon opened up to reveal an imposing stone wall stretching up into the sky. It was unnervingly high.

Arlo's mouth went dry as he stared at it. "What on earth is in there?"

"That's the giant's garden," Eleon answered casually, as if discussing an everyday garden rather than a massive, mysterious wall. "Do you want to see what's inside?"

Arlo felt a spark of interest, but he hesitated. "It seems like he doesn't want anyone going in there."

Eleon's eyes twinkled. "Not anyone, no. But it's open at the top. The wall's there to keep the curious out, bunnies and ground dwellers, but anyone who can fly is more than welcome."

Arlo furrowed his brow, skepticism creeping in. It didn't make much sense, but then again, this was a strange world. Maybe Eleon was telling the truth?

As they turned a corner, a slow-moving turtle appeared on the path ahead, so engrossed in its journey it didn't seem to notice the two of them approaching. "Boo!" A voice, as loud and eerie as a ghost's scream, echoed from beside the stone wall.

The turtle froze, then recoiled into its shell, startled by the sudden, unexpected sound.

A burst of laughter rang out from the wall, and Arlo saw another chameleon fade in, its body had been perfectly camouflaged against the stone. The prankster had been blending in so seamlessly Arlo hadn't even noticed him until now.

The turtle, hearing the laughter, cautiously peeked his head out of his shell, shot the chameleon a disapproving glare, and then hurried off.

Arlo wasn't sure if the prank was funny, but when Eleon erupted into laughter alongside the new chameleon, he began to wonder if this was just the way things were here, playful and lighthearted.

The two chameleons exchanged an odd, intricate handshake, something that seemed more like a series of gestures than a simple greeting. Then Eleon introduced his friend.

"Komo, this is Arlo. The flying lizard."

Arlo shook hands with him, though the weird hand shake threw him. Fortunately, it was confusing enough to keep Arlo from correcting them again and declaring he was a dragon.

As the three of them spoke, Arlo realized he wasn't entirely included in the conversation. They talked in cryptic tones, mentioning things that were clearly meant to leave him out of the loop. He almost excused himself, but then a sharp cry from above caught his attention.

A bird had been startled by another chameleon who attempted to land on its back. The bird banked sharply to the left as the lizard fell to the ground. The bird, barely recovering from the near collision, shot a furious chirp at the chameleon before soaring away, visibly displeased.

The chameleon landed with a roll, unfazed, and exchanged the same perplexing handshake with the others. Arlo was growing increasingly uncomfortable in their company.

"So," Eleon said, turning to him with a grin, "this is Arlo. He's going to fly us over the wall."

Arlo froze, his mouth falling open. "Wait— what?" he stammered, eyes wide with alarm.

When did I agree to that?

Kyrea had spent the morning going from one room to the next, searching every piece of furniture she could find. She began to wonder if the shoes would even still be in the stolen furniture. If the child would have opened the door or drawer and saw the shimmering shoes, she could only imagine what the child might do with them. Would she dump them out to play with them? But why? It's not like the child could fit in the shoes. Only dolls with really small feet could fit them.

She recalled the size of some of the action figures she had seen other children play with in the past. She imagined that not even the scale 8:1 would have fit those shoes. She glanced up at the many shelves of toys, stuffed animals and books. Nothing up there looked to be wearing those glittery shoes but there were plenty of places where they could have been placed. Small trinket boxes, a jewelry box, various bags and baskets... if the shoes weren't in the house, they could be elsewhere in the room. *Oh my...* Kyrea surmised, *this could get daunting.*

Oh, I hope they're still in this house somewhere.

She had scoured through nearly two-dozen rooms and was in the attic when she saw the giant's young daughter wake from her bed.

She may have only been a young child, but her giant size was simply massive to Kyrea's eyes. Kyrea was smaller than one of the girls' wiggly toes and she shivered at the thought of being found. Kyrea hid behind a rounded top storage trunk and watched the girl slowly slide out of bed.

She slipped on a pair of fuzzy slippers, stood and stretched and then ran over to her shelf and yanked a stuffed toy from it, cuddling it in her arms. Then she skipped to the door and left the room yelling down the hall, "I'm hungry!" Her voice bellowed and echoed loudly even though Kyrea was sure a giant's ears would have only heard a sweet little girl's coo. She sighed with relief and stood up.

Finishing her search in the attic she returned back downstairs. She retraced her steps, making sure she went through every room... well every room with furniture. Then it occurred to her, she hadn't checked the bathrooms. I mean, why would there be gemstone shoes in a bathroom? She walked in checked under the sink, looked inside the toilet then pulled back the shower curtain to the bath tub.

Her eyes sparkled like diamonds. Why the shoes were in the tub along with a box of jewelry and a gob of golden vases was beyond her comprehension, but here they were. Every sparkling, colorful trinket the young child found was collected in the bathtub.

Maybe she just wanted to keep all of the sparkly things together, maybe this tub doubled as a bowl to the young girl. To Kyrea, it didn't matter. She had found what she had come for.

She ran to the bedroom, ripped a pillowcase off of a pillow and returned to the bathroom where she began filling the pillowcase with treasures. She started with the shoes, making sure she collected both pairs of emerald slippers, sapphire stilettos, diamond Derbies and the golden boots. Then she sifted through the rest of the treasures. She grabbed large stone pendants, shimmery necklaces, golden goblets, and other shimmering treasures of value.

Kyrea had just finished tying the pillowcase tightly at the top and, with one swift motion, flung it over her shoulder. As she turned to leave, the sound of the door creaked open behind her. She froze. There, in the doorway, stood the young girl. She was staring at Kyrea as she entered the room.

Kyrea stood still, holding the bag against her side, watching the girl with a mix of curiosity and caution. *What was she thinking? Had she seen her? Was she even aware there was an intruder sneaking around in her dollhouse? Or was the girl simply looking at the dollhouse deciding if she wanted to play with it?*

The girl's attention, however, turned elsewhere. She skipped to the shelves, reached for a doll on her toy shelf, then turned back to the dollhouse. Sliding to her knees, she placed the doll in the bed that Kyrea had slept in and covered her up. Then she gazed into the bathroom where Kyrea was standing, still as a statue. Reaching for the tiny figure inside, Kyrea realized she could be in trouble.

Her heart skipped a beat. There was no way she could survive unscathed in the hands of this young giantess. Panic surged as she determined her escape. She sprinted across the room, her legs carrying her faster than she'd ever run before. Her pulse thudded in her ears as she leapt from the dollhouse's edge, barely missing the girl's hand.

The young girl, startled by Kyrea's sudden movement, rose quickly to her feet, her massive hands using the dollhouse as leverage to rise. Yet, her weight was too much for the dollhouse. The entire structure groaned and cracked, and with a loud *crash*, the attic collapsed to the floor.

For a moment, the chaos of the crash distracted the girl, pulling her focus away from Kyrea. The opportunity was slim, but it was all Kyrea needed. She was already halfway to the open door, the wide hall stretching out ahead of her.

The sound of heavy footsteps echoed behind her, she could hear the girl's movement, though it sounded muffled, as if the girl was still dealing with the debris of the dollhouse.

Then, out of the corner of her eye, Kyrea spotted something; the goose. It was waddling down the hall, unfazed by the commotion. Desperation flooded Kyrea's veins as she called to him, "Would you be willing to help me escape?"

The goose's eyes widened at the sound of her voice, but in an instant, his long wings stretched out to his side. Without hesitation, Kyrea ran up his wing as if it were a ramp. "Go!" She called out. "Go, Go!"

The goose flapped his wings as he ran, taking off with a burst of speed, running down the hall as the young giant's footsteps grew louder.

Kyrea's heart pounded harder as she glanced over her shoulder. She watched as the girl was closing in, but her towering form was barely able to maneuver around the obstacles in the hall.

The goose wasn't about to be caught, though. With a powerful thrust, it leaped into the air, soaring over chandeliers, past flickering wall torches, and darting through the castle's winding corridors. Kyrea's stomach twisted as she turned back to see the girl reach for them. Fortunately, her large hand slammed into the wall with a loud thud.

Kyrea's breath caught in her throat as they shot through an open window, the cold air rushing in. They were free. But the young girl wasn't about to let them go without a fight.

"Daddy!" she screamed, her voice piercing the air, but it was too late. Kyrea and the goose were already flying far beyond her grasp, soaring over the moat, past the drawbridge, and out into the open sky.

The castle was far behind them now, but Kyrea couldn't stop herself from glancing over her shoulder, feeling the weight of her escape pressing on her chest. The goose banked to the side and landed gracefully on the cobblestone street, bringing them safely back to solid ground.

Kyrea hopped off his back and thanked him profusely, her voice shaking with gratitude. "I don't know how I would have gotten out of there without you," she said, giving the goose a deep nod of appreciation. "You are my hero!"

With a final, brief farewell, she began walking down the street, her destination clear, their bean stalk, now visible again against the horizon.

She was a short trek into her walk when a loud bang echoed from behind her. The massive castle doors swung open with a force that rattled the air.

"Where is the thief?" The giant king's voice bellowed, booming loudly through the streets.

Kyrea's stomach dropped. *Uh-oh.* She gasped, her pace quickening as she sprinted towards the distant field, hoping the thick flowers and tall grass would hide her from view.

Her heart raced as she ran, glancing over her shoulder to make sure the king hadn't spotted her. Every step felt like it might be her last, but she had to keep moving. The beanstalk wasn't far, thanks to the goose. Freedom was just within her grasp.

As she ran, she felt something poking her. The sharp heel of the stiletto tearing a hole in the pillowcase, as the contents shifted inside. It didn't slow her down, though; if anything, it spurred her on. Each poke a painful pointy reminder of the urgency of her escape.

Somehow, the chameleons had managed to talk Arlo into flying them over the towering wall and into the giant's garden. Once they were in, they wasted no time. With gleeful chatter, they scampered straight to the plump, sun-ripened strawberries, sinking their tiny mouths into the soft red fruit.

Arlo hovered nearby, his large wings beating gently as he watched them feast. He felt a twinge of hunger himself, but something about this didn't sit quite right. The whole situation felt *off.*

"Come, friend!" one of the chameleons called, their eyes glittering with delight as they chewed, sweet red juice dripping down their chin. "Try one of these strawberries! They are delicious!"

Arlo hesitated, glancing down at the juicy fruit. His stomach growled, but the nagging sense of unease gnawed at him. *Should he indulge? Or should he just leave?*

Before he could decide, a booming voice shattered the calm of the garden. Arlo's head snapped around as the giant gardener emerged from the greenhouse. His face was red with rage, his massive hands clenched in fists. When he saw the scattered strawberry tops littering the ground and the chameleons happily munching away, his anger flared.

"I'll get you, you lizard thieves! No one eats the king's fruit except the king!"

The chameleons froze mid-bite, eyes widening in terror. They scrambled toward Arlo, their legs flailing as they tried to get to safety. But Arlo's wings twitched in frustration. He couldn't carry all three of them at once for fear of dropping them. Plus, the extra weight would slow him down, and he too, might get caught, or squashed.

A deep sense of responsibility gripped Arlo. *This was their decision. They had gotten themselves into this mess.* He couldn't risk getting caught, especially not for something he had not done. With a single powerful flap of his wings, he shot into the sky, soaring over the towering wall at breakneck speed.

"Now we have flying lizards?" the gardener groaned in disbelief, swatting the air above him like he could somehow catch Arlo mid-flight. His huge form shifted in frustration, but he turned his attention back to the three chameleons still scrambling for cover on the ground.

Arlo didn't look back, but as he glanced toward the horizon, he couldn't shake the feeling that he had just left a mess behind him, one that would only get worse before it got better.

Should he have left them? Should he go back?

If they get away they are going to hate Arlo for abandoning them. *This is not good.*

Maybe I should go check on Kyrea, I think my welcome here may be short-lived.

THE FALL FROM GIANT WORLD

The thick grass and dense shrubs made it nearly impossible for Kyrea to see the ground as she ran. The underbrush tangling with her feet, slowing her down. She could hear the heavy, thunderous footsteps of the giant echoing in the distance, getting closer as he raced across the drawbridge. There was no way she could outrun him.

Her thoughts were consumed by the question of *What am I going to do? How will I escape?* As she ran, her mind scrambled for a plan. Suddenly, her foot landed wrong, and her body jolted forward. She had no time to react. Before she could even register what was happening, the ground vanished beneath her, and she was falling; plummeting through a gap in the cloud world and free falling into oblivion.

Her heart leaped into her throat as she tumbled through the air, her stomach flipping with the sensation of the fall. She clenched the pillowcase full of shoes tightly in her hands, trying to steady herself.

Well, this could be a problem, Kyrea thought, spinning mid-air as the world above seemed to shrink farther and farther away.

The wind rushed past her as she somersaulted through the clouds, the terrifying realization sinking in that the only thing keeping her from certain disaster was the fact that she was immortal. The landing would hurt like nothing else, but death wasn't an option... *was it?* Still, the idea of slamming into the ground with all this speed... that was a thought she'd rather not dwell on.

But then, something caught her attention. A fleeting memory, a moment of clarity in the midst of chaos. *Arlo.* When she'd first met him, he had told her if she ever needed help, all she had to do was whistle. *Well, this precise moment certainly qualifies*, Kyrea decided.

With a new spark of hope, Kyrea spread her lips and pressed her two fingers to her mouth, to make a whistle. She inhaled deeply, gathering all the air she could. She put all her energy into the sharp, ear-splitting whistle which cut through the air like a crack of thunder. The sound seemed to ripple outward, as if it was swallowed by the sky itself, with no walls to bounce off of.

She waited. Nothing.

Kyrea's stomach lurched as the ground was inevitably moving closer. Panic started to claw at her, but she refused to give in. Taking another breath, she whistled again, this time even louder, more desperate. The air around her seemed to hum with the intensity of the sound. She squeezed her eyes shut, hoping beyond reason that Arlo would hear her.

As the wind whipped through her hair and the dizzying drop continued, she closed her eyes, surrendering to the feeling of freefall, all the while trying to ignore the unsettling thought of what the impact would be like when she finally hit the ground.

Arlo soared through the air, his wings cutting through the wind as he scanned the horizon. That's when he noticed, the large green stalk had reappeared. It stood tall and proud, piercing the sky like a giant's ladder reaching for the heavens. Intrigued, Arlo began flying towards it, but then, he heard *a whistle*.

A high-pitched, almost frantic sound sliced through the air and straight into Arlo's ears. The whistle, sounded strangely familiar.

Wait... that's...

Another sharp whistle followed. This one had a sense of urgency to it. Arlo's heart skipped a beat. It sounded like Kyrea was in trouble.

Without a second thought, Arlo snapped his wings and began hurtling toward the sound. He passed the towering vine, shot through the hole in the cloud world, and dove into the open sky beneath.

His sharp eyes swept the horizon. The vast white and blue expanse stretched on forever. And then, there she was. Kyrea. Freefalling. Her body spiraling through the air, miles above the ground.

No time to waste.

Arlo's wings beat faster, and he dove like a comet streaking through the sky. His heart pounded in his chest as he hurtled toward her, his voice booming across the wind.

"Kyrea! I'm coming!"

She looked up just in time to see him racing toward her, a relieved smile spread across her face. She waved at him, still holding the pillowcase tightly in her hands, despite the terrifying plummet.

Arlo closed the distance between them with tremendous speed. The wind rushed beneath him like a powerful current as he passed her with a burst of force, his wings sending a shockwave of air around them both. He slowed as he arced back up beneath her, his massive wings flaring wide.

With one final swoop, Arlo raised himself underneath Kyrea, catching her on his back. The impact was rough. She landed hard against his scales, and nearly slipped off, but at least she was safe. The sudden shock of the landing made the world around her blur for a moment, but she was alive.

However, the pillowcase had not been so lucky. The shoes and contents had jostled and shifted during her desperate run, and the sharp stiletto's heel had poked a small hole in the fabric.

A small sparkling necklace slipped through the hole, glittering in the air as it tumbled free.

Kyrea tried to reach for it but it was in vain. The smoothly polished ruby red amulet strung on a short thin gold chain had slipped through the hole and was tumbling away from her grasp. It was already well out of her reach. It shimmered with a pulse that seemed to carry an ancient knowledge or some obscure hidden power, but Kyrea didn't dare ask Arlo to go after it. She was simply grateful he came for her when he did!

She watched helplessly as it vanished into the abyss below. She wondered briefly what it was, what it could do? Maybe someday it will be found. Maybe they will write a book about it? Though, the ruby red amulet was small, so small it looked like it could only fit around a mouse's neck... or a rat.

Destroying the Beanstalk

The next morning, Arlo awoke to the familiar scent of gingerbread which always lingered inside the warm, little cabin. After a night of rest following their adventure in the Giant World, it felt strange to wonder what they were going to do today.

With a stretch and yawn, Arlo grabbed his stack of books from beside his bed and walked across the room. His claws tapped against the wooden floor as he made his way to the purple-bordered door of the library. He knocked three times and watched the purple illumination create a three-dimensional door that he could open. The sight was always fascinating to him. After returning the books to their proper shelves, he returned to the cabin and closed the door.

Stepping outside, the morning light shining through the trees, he spotted Kyrea standing by the vine. Kyrea had been out there for hours, her small frame dwarfed by the towering vine, her focus intense. She stood with her arms stretched high, eyes narrowed with concentration, and a fierce purpose etched across her face. A trail of moisture swirled around her, pulling at the tendrils of the vine like invisible threads.

"What are you doing?" Arlo asked, his voice carrying across the still morning air.

Kyrea didn't even glance at him, her focus on the vine. "I'm shrinking it," she said, her tone quiet but unwavering. "I need to pull the moisture from the vine so that when I cut it down, it won't pummel everything underneath it. If it stays this heavy, it could crush the house and a good section of the woods. If the moisture is extracted, it'll be a lot lighter."

Arlo's eyebrow lifted. "Shrinking? How do you…"

"Water manipulation," she interrupted his train of thought, her hands lifting higher. "I pull out the liquid inside and spread it across the garden. When the vine's lighter, it'll fall harmlessly."

Arlo watched her for a moment, intrigued by her quiet power. "How long do you think this will take?"

"A few more hours," Kyrea muttered, sweat beading on her forehead despite the cool morning breeze. "I'm tired, though. I may need a break soon."

He stepped closer, glancing at the still-growing vine. "Isn't there another way we could do this without risking the house?"

Kyrea paused, a glint of mischief in her eyes as she turned toward him. "Well, I *did* consider setting it on fire."

Arlo blinked. "Isn't that a bit extreme?"

Kyrea shrugged. "Fire would burn it down fast, but then I'd risk burning the forest, the house, maybe even the whole valley."

"Traditional fire can't be controlled, true," Arlo said, the corners of his mouth twitching upward. "But there is another kind."

Kyrea tilted her head. "Another kind?"

Arlo grinned, showing his teeth. "Dragon fire."

The mention of it made Kyrea's eyes light up, her face broke into a wide smile. "That's genius! If you could fly above the forest canopy and start the fire up there, it would burn upwards, and the vine's growth would stop. Everything else would burn away, turning to ash."

"And I could control the fire so it doesn't spread to the trees below," Arlo added.

Kyrea nodded, excitement building. "Exactly! While you handle that, I can finish draining the lower part of the vine and keep it from being too heavy when it falls. Then, when you're done, I'll cut it down carefully, and it won't be a problem."

"I like it," Arlo said, stretching his wings. "But first..." He wandered over to the apple tree, plucked a branch heavy with fruit, and tossed it over to Kyrea.

"Breakfast," he said, grinning. "It's the most important meal of the day."

Kyrea smiled as she took an apple. She bit into it, her eyes bright. "Thank you, my friend."

After a brief but needed pause, Kyrea returned to her task. Arlo watched her for a moment before stretching out his wings. With a heavy flap, he rose into the sky, soaring higher and higher until the ground below seemed a distant memory. As the air thinned and the clouds loomed closer, he inhaled deeply, preparing himself. Then, with a burst of searing heat, Arlo exhaled a stream of dragon fire which shot upward, engulfing the vine.

Flames raced along the length of the vine, creeping skyward like an unstoppable wave of heat. The vine began to writhe and twist as the fire consumed it, turning the plant to ash. Arlo hovered, watching the beautiful chaos unfold.

He wasn't done yet.

Flying lower, just above the treetops, he exhaled another focused burst of dragon fire. The blaze burned clean and fast, consuming the rest of the vine in a controlled inferno that left behind only faint wisps of smoke and ash.

Kyrea, still working below, pulled the last of the moisture from the vine's trunk, redirecting it to the trees around them. The forest seemed to breathe a little deeper, the plants and trees swelling with new life as the water nourished the earth.

When Arlo returned to the ground, the vine had shrunk significantly, its once-massive bulk reduced to a thin dried-up twig. He then burst a short flame up the stalk using his wings to keep it fanned and low. He hovered over the pile, ensuring the fire didn't flare back to life, and directed a soft puff of dragon fire to burn the remaining embers at its roots. It was done. The vine was gone, nothing but a pile of blackened ash remained to be scattered by the wind.

Kyrea grabbed a shovel and began digging down to check for any remaining roots. "I'd rather make sure it's all gone," she said, her face serious as she worked. "Don't want it starting to grow again after we are gone."

Once she was satisfied, she wiped her brow and stood up. "Done."

Arlo chuckled. "That wasn't so bad. What should we do now?"

Kyrea turned, brushing off her hands. "Well, I have to return the princess's shoes to the palace."

Arlo's face fell at the thought of humans and castles. "You're asking *me* to go to a castle?"

Kyrea raised an eyebrow, the smile never leaving her face. "I didn't expect you to come inside, but *maybe* you could fly me nearby? I can walk the rest of the way."

Arlo sighed, but his wings twitched in anticipation. "Fine. But I'm not going anywhere near those humans… and I'm going to want to bring a book to read."

"Deal," Kyrea grinned, as they headed into the house. "I'll just grab the bag, then we can go."

"Where are we going?" Arlo inquired as he reached for his book.

"Evershade, it's a wonderous castle nestled between a great mountain range which can only be accessed by traversing over a pathway of floating disks. It's a beautiful place I hear."

"You've never been there?" Arlo inquired.

"Nope. I've only ever read about it. So I cannot wait to visit it and meet the princess and her family!"

The

Kingdom

of

Evershade

$\mathcal{A}$RLO CIRCLED THE SKY ONCE, his wings stretching as he hovered, then gently descended. He dropped Kyrea off just outside the kingdom, and remained hidden in the shadows of the forest's edge. He gave her a nod of reassurance.

"I promise I won't be long," she said, placing the pillowcase full of the princess's magical shoes on the ground beside her.

"It's fine," Arlo said, settling into the trees. "Take your time. I brought a book." He reached under his scales, pulling out the book with a smirk.

Kyrea arched an eyebrow. "Did you keep that from the library?"

"They had two copies," Arlo replied with a mischievous grin. "But I figured when I'm done, you can just draw me another door, right?"

"Would you like to hold onto the purple crayon? Just in case you need to go anywhere?"

"That would be wonderful!" Arlo smiled brightly as Kyrea tossed the crayon to him from her side bag. He placed it under one of his armored chest plates and patted it with a smile, showing her that it was safe where it was.

Kyrea smiled warmly at him. "Would you mind if I stayed for dinner? I have a feeling they will ask."

"Not a problem, stay the night if you want. This book is going to take me a while to finish." Arlo held up the thick book. There was a man in reddish purple standing on a metallic contraption surrounded by an ocean on the front cover.

Kyrea recognized the nearly 400-page book and smirked at the dragon's choice. "You'll enjoy the story." She grinned, then tossed the pillowcase over her shoulder again. "I'll be back soon." She called out as she began walking toward the kingdom gates.

"Take your time." Arlo hummed, his nose already deep within the pages.

As Kyrea arrived at the castle's gate, she announced her arrival to the guards. They escorted her through the grand stone archways, and as they entered the castle's bustling courtyard, the princess herself appeared, graceful and radiant, with a curious smile on her face.

"I found your diary, Princess Winddiac" Kyrea began, stepping forward with a curtsy, her voice soft yet steady. "And I have to admit... I read it."

The princess's eyes widened. "My diary? I lost it so long ago... I thought the ogres had it."

Kyrea chuckled. "Oh, they did. I was able to trade something to get it back for you."

"Well, thank you," the princess said, eyes brightening. "I'll gladly pay you back for whatever it was you traded."

Kyrea shook her head, waving away the offer. "You don't need to worry about that. But I did read something which caught my attention. It seems a giant kept pulling the roof off the castle and stealing the kingdom's furniture."

The princess laughed lightly, a touch of exasperation in her voice. "Yes, that was quite odd and unnerving. He'd taken enough furniture to fill an entire house... but after a while, he just stopped."

"I know," Kyrea replied. "He was furnishing a dollhouse for his daughter."

"A dollhouse?" The princess blinked in surprise.

"Yes," Kyrea continued. "But I also read in your diary that one of the pieces of furniture contained your magical shoes."

The princess's face grew serious at the mention of her shoes. "You read that too?"

"I did," Kyrea confirmed. "So, I went up to the Giant World, found the dollhouse, and retrieved them for you." She gently pulled the pillowcase from her shoulder and opened it up to reveal the sparkling shoes.

The princess gasped, her eyes lighting up as she looked at the emerald slippers and sapphire stilettos shimmering in the sunlight. "You have no idea how happy this has made me..." She spotted the diamond derbies and her mom's golden boots. "How happy my parents will be!" She rushed forward and wrapped Kyrea in a tight hug, her voice full of gratitude. "This means so much to us."

Kyrea smiled; her voice warm. "I just wanted to help." She did feel very satisfied by the reception.

Princess Winddiac stepped back, still grinning. "You must let me offer you something in return for your heroism! Come! Come inside! You need to meet my parents. Is there anything you want? You must stay the night! We should throw a massive feast in your honor!"

Kyrea raised a hand. "I've heard the castle has quite an amazing library…. I love to read."

"Well, by all means!" The princess's eyes sparkled with excitement. "Please. Help yourself! Stay as long as you want. In fact, if I have any books you'd be interested in, you're welcome to take them with you." She was overjoyed someone else liked books as much as she did.

The princess led Kyrea through a grand hall, and with a flourish, opened the door to the royal library. Kyrea's breath caught in her chest as she stepped into the room, the shelves stacked high with books, their spines glistening in the soft light. The room was rich with the scent of parchment and wood.

Kyrea couldn't visibly hide her awe. "This is incredible," she gushed, eyes wide with wonder.

They chatted for a while, the princess guiding her to the books she thought Kyrea would enjoy. As Kyrea scoured the shelves, gathering a few treasured choices in her arms, she asked the princess a few questions. "By chance, have you ever heard of any magician or creature that could grant wishes or save someone's life?"

The princess paused and thought about it. "I assume you know about genies granting wishes?"

"Oh yes." Kyrea nodded, "anything else, maybe a fairy tale told in your kingdom?"

"Not that I can think of. Unicorns maybe. Though I'm fairly certain they perform miracles, not just grant wishes."

"You're right, they're quite special." Kyrea smiled brightly having met a few unicorns in her time.

The princess spoke again. "Well, I guess I'll leave you to read. Stay as long as you like, of course. And I insist you stay for dinner. My parents are going to love meeting you!"

Kyrea placed her stack of books on a nearby table. "That sounds amazing. Thank you so much!"

MEANWHILE, IN THE FOREST...

Hidden deep in the forest, Arlo had found a quiet spot beneath the shade of an ancient oak tree. There, he settled himself comfortably, sprawled out on the forest floor with the book in his claws. He was absorbed in its pages; his thoughts consumed with the wonders of the ocean.

Even in the opening chapters, the book hinted at expansive underwater realms and strange creatures. Whispers of sea monsters and the mysteries of the deep Arlo's heart longed to see an underwater world. He was fascinated by it all, though he knew it was unlikely he would ever get to explore the ocean. He had a persistent fear ocean water could douse his dragon fire, a risk he'd never take.

Curiously, he stopped reading for a moment and wondered aloud, "What *is* a league? How far down would 20,000 leagues be?"

His eyes narrowed as he tried to calculate the depth. *A league is 3 miles. Times 20,0000 would be...* "That's 60,000 miles! Why that's... that's absolutely preposterous! The tallest mountain on earth is Everest and it's less than 6 miles tall!"

Now wondering how realistic the story would be; Arlo felt a bit of doubt. Surely the author didn't mean it literally? He was happy when he learned that they traveled sixty thousand miles around the ocean.

He turned the page, eager to discover more though. The idea of submerged cities, treasures untold, and ocean creatures in a world he had never seen, filled his imagination. His imagination was hardly enough to contain it. *Oh how he wished to see the depths of the ocean with his own two eyes...*

Kyrea spent the afternoon scouring the library of Evershade Castle investigating every unknown book she could find. The library was fabulous; three stories tall, with rolling ladders available for every section. She explored the books on the top shelves, the ones with inches worth of dust accumulated on them, the ones that hadn't been read in ages as she knew they contained knowledge long lost to others.

She enjoyed her time, but kept an eye on the setting sun. As it began to beam in through the stained-glass windows, Kyrea, put aside the book she was flipping through and walked to the fantasy section. There she located a reddish-brown cloth book with a gold emblem on the front. It was an outlined picture of a girl holding a pig in her arms like a baby. She checked the date on the copyright page, 1865, and then proudly flipped to the second chapter. There she found the illustration she desired.

She reached into the book and pulled out a bottle labeled "DRINK ME" then placed it in her side bag. Then she did it again, removing a second bottle. She did it twice more to remove two pieces of cake that she placed into a container and also slipped into her side bag. She then replaced the book on the shelf and returned to the book she had been reading.

About half an hour later the princess walked in. "Sorry to bother you, but would you like to join us for dinner, now?"

Kyrea smiled brightly and stood up, placing a finger in the book to mark her spot. "May I come back here after dinner to finish reading?"

"Of course! You're welcome to stay the night, I can have a chambermaid ready a guestroom for you."

Kyrea looked at her thoughtfully and then said, I know this may sound odd, but a pillow and blanket here would make me the happiest girl in the world."

"No, my friend, I am the happiest girl as you found my magical shoes. If this is all you want for such a heroic task, it is yours, and you are welcome to return any time you want." The princess then untied a ribbon from her dress and handed it to Kyrea. Confused Kyrea cocked her head to the side. "For the book, to mark your place."

"Brilliant." Kyrea smiled as she accepted the ribbon. Carefully placing it in between the pages of the book, she laid it on the side table and joined the princess as they made their way to the dining hall.

THE FEAST

IN THE GRAND DINING HALL, Kyrea saw a long table stretched beneath towering candlelit chandeliers, with dishes piled high on silver platters. The savory aromas of smoked ham, spiced vegetables, and freshly baked bread filled the air, mingling with the laughter of the royal family. They had already welcomed Kyrea into the fold, and now, the feast began in earnest.

The princess sat within the middle section of the table, a radiant smile on her face as she gestured to the platters in front of her. Kyrea felt both honored and humbled by the grandeur of the meal, her senses alive with every mouth-watering scent.

"So, Kyrea," the king boomed, his deep voice warm and inviting. "Tell us more about yourself. My daughter tells me you've traveled to the Giant World?"

Kyrea smiled, her eyes reflecting the firelight. "I have a unique desire to explore realms and meet all creatures known to man. I've spent my life learning about the mystical and traveling to far-off places. It's been a true joy."

The king let out a hearty laugh, slapping the table. "Spent your life? But you're just a child! Hardly even in your teens. How could you have spent your life traveling to all these grand places?"

Kyrea's smile deepened with a coy look in her eyes. "Don't let my appearance fool you. I am much older than I look."

The king's eyes twinkled with amusement, and the princess laughed along. Kyrea's stories had enchanted them, though she could sense their disbelief. That was okay though, she didn't need to convince them. Their gratitude and hospitality was enough for her.

As the evening wore on, Kyrea found herself drawn to a tapestry hanging on the far wall. It depicted an intricate map of ancient lands, realms unknown, and forgotten kingdoms. It was beautiful and mysterious, and something about it stirred a quiet longing inside her.

With a thoughtful glance, she committed the tapestry to memory, knowing one day—perhaps sooner than she expected—she would return. There was still much to discover in this strange and wonderful world.

Kyrea returned to the forest from the princess's castle the next afternoon. As she walked, her eyes scanned the woodland, until she saw him. Arlo was seated under an ancient oak, leaning against its gnarled trunk. His golden eyes were engrossed in the same thick book, his tail idly swishing the ground in slow arcs. She recognized this movement from her own times reading when her leg would bounce as something good was happening.

Kyrea smiled to herself; her heart warmed by the sight of her happy friend. She slid a satchel from her shoulder and unfurled it next to Arlo. The sack was filled with a bounty from the castle, freshly baked breads, ripe fruits, and tangy cheeses. She then sat down on the other side of the food.

The moment the aromas reached Arlo's nostrils, his attention shifted. He reached down, almost without thinking, and snatched a handful of food with his large, clawed fingers. His gaze stayed locked on the book in his paws as he tossed the food into his mouth, chewing idly, as though the words on the page held more allure than the feast laid out at his side.

After swallowing, he reached down again for more, this time plucking a loaf of bread from the assortment. He tore it in half with one swift motion and tossed it into his mouth, not missing a beat with his reading.

"Thank you, Kyrea," he said, his voice rumbling like distant thunder, though his eyes never left the page. The words were warm and thoughtful, but the focus of his mind was still lost in the pages of his book. Kyrea chuckled softly, her gaze turning inward as she unstrapped her side bag and carefully pulled out the copper coin with the square hole that she had been carrying since the garden at Yorkshire Moore.

It gleamed faintly in the dimming light, casting small, iridescent reflections onto the surrounding leaves. She held it up, letting its ethereal glow dance in the fading sun. It was definitely not of this world. Its craftsmanship was too refined, its symbols too intricate. Kyrea squinted at the tiny, elegant runes engraved on the surface. There was something deeply mystical about it, something she could almost *feel*, yet the meanings of the symbols eluded her. No matter how hard she tried, they were too small to make sense of. She pulled a magnifying glass from her pouch she had acquired from the castle.

She held the small copper coin up to the light, peering through the magnifying glass with wide eyes. As the lens sharpened the tiny etchings, she recognized the shapes. These markings were from the fairy world. *That's what I expected,* Kyrea confirmed in her mind. Sighing, Kyrea placed the medallion on her lap and returned the magnifying glass back into her pouch.

She had long suspected the etchings belonged to mystical beings far smaller than herself, but now, through the magnifying glass, she had confirmed it was indeed fairy writing. She was glad she'd acquired the shrinking potion while she was in the kingdom's library, the one she'd stored carefully in her belt pouch. She had suspected they would need to shrink down to fairy size when the time came to return the medallion. But a larger question loomed: *Where* would they need to go? Which fairy realm would hold the answers they sought?

Her fingers moved absent-mindedly as she clasped her hands together and spread them apart, her movements precise as she opened a tiny, glowing portal before her. The air shimmered as the portal expanded. Then, reaching inside, she collected and pulled out a medium-sized book with intricate golden filigree spiraling around its edges. The cover, adorned with three-dimensional, sparkling fairy wings, which softly fluttered with a hazy glow. A cursive "F" appeared on the front, the letter delicate and shimmering as though it were made of starlight.

The soft sparkle of magic caught Arlo's attention. His golden eyes looked up from his book, his left eyebrow arching in silent curiosity.

"It's the Oracle of Fairy Realms," Kyrea answered before he could voice the question. She gave him a knowing smile, her lips curling slightly.

Arlo nodded thoughtfully, having seen her pull books from magical portals many times now, though it always amazed him to watch. "One day you may need to teach me how you do that."

Kyrea thought about it for a moment, then spoke, *"I might be able to do that..."*

Arlo's eyes though, returned to his book. He knew it wasn't going to happen right now and he was so close to finishing the story.

Kyrea, too, began her reading, the soft rustle of pages filling the air around them.

She didn't need to look up to know where Arlo was in the story, his emotions were so visible to her.

His shoulders tensed, and his eyes widened with excitement as he read about the submarine's daring journey. She could see his body relax as the narrative shifted, his face reflecting the thrill of adventure, then sinking into somberness as the crew faced uncertainty. She could almost feel his emotions, she knew where in the story he was as she observed him. When Arlo flipped the page and sighed deeply, she knew he had reached the chapter where the submarine faced its greatest challenge.

She smiled softly. The end of an adventure was always bittersweet. She had watched him experience this countless times, and knew how the pages of a story could pull at one's heart with the weight of loss, only to give way to reflection and closure once the final words were read.

As Arlo's eyes lingered on the last page, Kyrea turned her attention back to her own book. The Oracle spoke of many things, of magic and realms beyond counting, but one particular tale had caught her eye. The fairies were said to possess artifacts of immense power, objects that allowed them to travel between realms, transcending boundaries. She was drawn to one of these objects in particular, an artifact she felt a strange, pull towards. Yet… this was not the answer she sought regarding the medallion.

Turning the page, her breath caught as the words revealed the secrets of the *Ethereal Gardens*. Everything clicked into place, like the final piece of a long-unsolved puzzle. The medallion was the key they had lost long ago. Kyrea's pulse quickened as she realized this was no ordinary quest.

She had known from the moment she first laid eyes on the medallion that it was not of this world, and now she understood why. She had to return it to the faeries, and she now knew exactly where to go.

Arlo closed his book with a soft snap. For a long moment, he remained still, his golden eyes fixed on the leaves above, lost in the silence of the forest. Kyrea, meanwhile, was scribbling notes, planning their next move. She knew Arlo was processing the story, savoring the feeling of stepping out of an extraordinary tale, but she also knew he would soon be eager to dive into another one.

Finally, Arlo broke the stillness. "That was a fabulous story," he said, his voice thoughtful, his expression lingering with adventure.

Kyrea smiled, setting her book aside for the moment. "I remember reading that story, it was a great adventure," she agreed, her fingers brushing against the medallion as her mind raced ahead to their next journey.

For a while, they talked about the story, exchanging thoughts on the characters and the twists of fate that had shaped the tale. But then, with a gleam of excitement in his eyes, Arlo turned the conversation toward her. "So... what have you been working on?"

Kyrea's smile widened. "Our next adventure, if you're interested in joining me."

His eyes lit up. "A new adventure?!" He practically bounced in place. "Where are we going? Please don't say another human town."

She smiled brightly. "Nope. We're heading to the fairy realm."

"Fairies?" Arlo repeated the word, unbelieving.

"Yes," Kyrea said, her voice filled with wonder. "And this is going to be incredible. We need to get to Aeloria, the land of the fairies. More specifically, the *Ethereal Gardens*."

Arlo's gaze sharpened, the hint of awe in his expression. "The Ethereal Gardens," he repeated slowly, the name rolling off his tongue like a secret. "That sounds like a beautiful adventure."

"I hope it will be," Kyrea said with conviction. "And it's going to be one like no other."

AELORIAN

FAIRIES

"WE'RE HERE!" Kyrea exclaimed brightly as the two on them came in for a landing in a secluded field. The grass was hip-height and tan. The trees blocked most of the morning sun. There were no flowers. No mushrooms, no little fairy houses…

Arlo felt a pang of disappointment. "It's just an empty field," he said, his golden eyes scanning the horizon. "Where are the fairies?"

Kyrea smiled, as though she'd been expecting this. "They're much smaller than we are. We need to shrink down to their size in order to see them."

Arlo's brow furrowed. "And how exactly are we going to do that?" He asked, as though he'd caught her off guard with a question she couldn't answer.

With a calm, assured motion, Kyrea pulled out two small glass bottles from her side bag. "With these." She held them up for Arlo to see.

Arlo took one of the bottles, inspecting it with a raised eyebrow. He read the label which said, "DRINK ME" and shrugged his shoulders trustfully.

Half-skeptical, half-amused, he uncorked the bottle and downed its contents in one sip. Within seconds, he began to shrink before Kyrea's eyes, his form contracting until he was no taller than the height of her big toe.

Kyrea smiled, shaking her head with a touch of amusement that he so quickly and willingly drank something unknown to him. She moved carefully, making sure not to step on him, and placed the medallion on a rock beside her. Then, with a soft exhale, she drank the potion herself. As she shrank, she marveled at how her surroundings seemed to grow larger, each blade of grass now towering over her like a tree, the air thick with the scent of earth and the hum of distant creatures.

Once she had fully shrunk, Kyrea found Arlo already scanning their new, enlarged surroundings. He looked at her, his face full of disappointment.

"Oh great!" he grumbled, his voice small but still familiar. "I just came from a giant world where I felt tiny. And now I'm small again?"

Kyrea's lips twitched in sympathy.

Arlo let out a sigh. "It's just... not as cool as being really big and powerful."

Kyrea chuckled softly. "I'm sorry, Arlo."

"It's fine," he said, shaking his head. "This should still be a fun adventure. At least I'm larger than you still." He pointed out with a cheshire grin.

AELORIA, THE FAERY REALM

THE MAJESTIC GATES OF AELORIA, the fairy city, came into view. A soft hum of enchantment grew louder, resonating with the pulse of the land itself. The gates stood tall and impossibly beautiful, covered with vines that shimmered with soft golden light, and adorned with flowers that seemed to change color as the wind passed through them. Kyrea approached the gates with a sense of purpose, her heart racing in anticipation. She knocked, the sound echoing strangely in the ethereal quiet.

A fairy guard flew down from above, his wings glittering in the sunlight, his features sharp with curiosity. He hovered before them, examining the pair closely. "What is your business here?" he asked, his voice a melodic trill which carried the weight of both authority and ancient grace.

"I need to speak with your town leader, please," Kyrea replied, her tone sure as her demeanor.

The guard's eyes narrowed, a gaze of suspicion crossing his face. "What is this regarding?"

"I believe I have found the Aureliax Medallion,"

The guard's expression shifted from suspicion to something more wary, then he gave a small nod. Without another word, he darted upward, disappearing into the air as swiftly as a passing breeze. Moments later, the great gates slowly opened with the sound of a distant chime. Kyrea and Arlo were welcomed in.

They moved quickly through the glittering streets of Aeloria, fairies gliding gracefully around them, their wings leaving behind trails of soft sparkle. Yet, what should have been a dazzling dream felt strangely... ordinary. The flowers, mushrooms, even the tiny tree houses nestled in the branches — they all looked like natural forest growth, not the enchanted wonders Kyrea had imagined.

She had read stories of glowing blossoms, bioluminescent mushrooms, and magical light that would dance across the leaves. In her mind, the fairy realm shimmered like a world bathed in stardust. But here, even with the sun catching the fairies' wings, they just looked... busy. Not joyful, not playful — just another part of nature. Kyrea couldn't understand it. Why did this magical place feel so normal?

Kyrea couldn't understand why it seemed so... *not dreary*, just... *not magical.*

Eventually, they arrived at a large conservatory, a majestic structure built of intertwining glass and vine, where the scent of rare blossoms and fresh earth filled the air. The door to the conservatory opened, and without a word, the fairy guard motioned for Kyrea to enter.

Arlo, was unsure of the surroundings, and hesitated at the door. "I'll wait out here," he said, his voice deep but not unfriendly.

"Okay, Arlo," Kyrea replied, giving him a reassuring smile before stepping inside. The door closed softly behind her, leaving Arlo alone.

At first, Arlo stood still, watching the door as he kept his senses sharp, every nerve alert. But his solitude didn't last long. Soon, a group of curious young fairies appeared, fluttering around him like a swarm of brightly colored butterflies. Their wings sparkled like liquid rainbows in the sunlight, and their high-pitched laughter filled the air.

"What is *that*?" one fairy asked, pointing at his massive form with wide eyes.

"I'm a dragon," Arlo rumbled.

"I have never seen a *dragonfly* like you before."

"That is because I am not a dragonfly, I am a dragon who can fly. He unfurled his large wings and flapped them once rising just above the ground for a moment before landing again.

The fairies blinked, clearly fascinated. One flew closer, her wings beating in rapid excitement. "Oh, that's fascinating" the same fairy giggled, hovering in front of him and flapping her wings furiously, causing a small gust of wind to ripple through the air.

Arlo's heart lightened as he watched their carefree antics. He had always been known for his imposing presence, but something about these tiny, bright creatures made him feel less like an intimidating force and more like a gentle giant. The fairies flittered around him, asking questions, offering him tiny flowers and leaves, and making him laugh with their innocence. His apprehension faded, replaced by a sense of joy.

Another fairy, her wings shimmering with a like crystal, darted around his tail. "Can you do tricks?" she asked excitedly.

Arlo's eyes gleamed. "Well," he said, stretching his wings with a flourish, "I can do a *few* things."

As he began to show off with a few playful aerial flips and somersaults, the fairies gasped in delight. Arlo's large form was surprisingly graceful in the air, his movements fluid despite his size. They cheered him on, their laughter ringing like chimes as they danced around him, thoroughly enchanted by the sight of a dragon soaring above them with ease.

Through it all, Arlo felt something he hadn't felt in a long time: a deep connection to the magic of this world. The fairies, so full of life and light, had a way of making everything feel happier, more joyful. For once, his imposing size wasn't something to fear, but something to celebrate.

INSIDE THE CONSERVATORY, the air was thick with the scent of blooming flowers, their petals glowing with a soft haze. It was as if they were magical but just barely. Kyrea's footsteps echoed softly against the marble floors as she approached an elder fairy, his wings bent and frayed with age, his long white hair flowing like silken threads around his fragile form. His eyes, though clouded with time, held a sharpness that belied his years.

He met her gaze as he studied her. "You said you had found the Aureliax?" he asked, his voice hopeful yet full of ancient wisdom.

Kyrea stood a little taller in the face of his scrutiny. "I did. Or at least, I think I did. It's copper in color, octagonal, with a square hole in the middle. The outer edges have a screw-like channel for something to be set on it, it seems. The etchings, though small, is what led me here."

The elder's gaze softened slightly, though he was still silent, waiting for more. "Where did you find it?" he asked, his tone gentle but filled with the weight of decades worth of hope and curiosity.

"Quite a distance away from here, in a fountain," Kyrea explained, her voice steady but filled with the reverence of the moment. "It took a great deal of research to figure out what it might be and where it should be returned. I hope I'm right."

The elder studied her closely, his expression unreadable, before he asked, "Where is it?"

"I left it outside, on a rock nearby," Kyrea said, a slight frown tugging at her lips. "It would have been too large for me to carry myself after we shrunk down to this size and I did not want it to shrink down with us for fear of altering its form."

The fairy elder nodded, signaling to a group of fairy guards who were hovering nearby. Without a word, they darted out of the conservatory to retrieve the medallion. As they departed, the elder's attention returned to Kyrea. His eyes held a deep sadness, as though recalling an ancient, bittersweet memory.

He began to speak, his voice low and almost distant. "This medallion, if it *is* the Aureliax, is a very important piece of our magical gardens," he started his story. "Without it, our magic is all but lost." His gnarled fingers reached up, tracing the air as if following the shape of an invisible story. "Many generations ago, a human passed through this area. Though we are shielded by our invisibility cloak, and he never saw us, his shoe accidentally kicked a small, inconspicuous object. He didn't know what it was, but he must have noticed the medallion, or the coin to use a word from your world. He picked it up, looked at it and then slid it into his pocket before continuing to walk away."

Kyrea's brow furrowed as she considered this.

"He was long gone before we realized what had happened and none of our scout fairies ever found him or the medallion."

Kyrea nodded her understanding while staying quiet so he could continue his history lesson.

"The medallion is used to complete a special centerpiece, a totem pole type of structure, that stands at the heart of our town. It is the focus of our magic. The medallion is needed to power the central platform, which in turn supports the magical crystal sphere that provides the light to grow our enchanted flowers." His voice broke slightly, as though the weight of his words was almost too much to bear.

"Without the medallion, the flowers stopped blooming, and the magical energy that once electrified our world, began to disappear. The magic from all worlds, began to fade."

Kyrea felt the gravity of his words. The magic was disappearing. She could feel it in the air around her. It was even a possible explanation of why the fairy kingdom didn't look as she had read and expected. And now, they just may have the key again to restore it.

Just then, the fairy guards returned. Their tiny wings fluttering in a chorus of sound as they flew back into the conservatory. They were carrying the Aureliax Medallion, all four fairies held a section of it. It dwarfed them and looked massive and heavy in comparison. Kyrea wondered how they could even lift such a large object... but then again, fairies were a lot like ants – stronger than they look.

The elder rushed forward, his movements surprisingly swift for one so old. He inspected the medallion with careful hands, his eyes scanning the intricate engravings etched into the copper. He ran his fingers over the symbols, reading the transcription as if unlocking an ancient language only he could understand. After a long moment, he nodded to the guards, his voice clear and authoritative.

"Take it," he instructed, "Fly it to the top of the pole. It's time to regain our magical fairy dust!"

CFRENZY OF GLITTER BLOOM

The guards nodded with bright smiles and quickly darted outside. The Aureliax Medallion gleamed in the light as they flew toward the towering totem pole at the center of Aeloria. All the fairies stopped what they were doing and turned to stare at it. Sparkling chatter and gasps of excitement filled the air as everyone fluttered by, awaiting the transformation of growth.

Arlo also turned to watch as the fairies buzzed by him. Kyrea walked out next to the elder and they both watched in awe as the medallion was placed at the very top of the pole, slid down to a gold-leaf stopper, and magically leveled itself. They clicked it into place, and suddenly everyone heard a soft, resonant hum rise up from the land.

Just then a group of about a dozen fairies emerged from another floral building, they combined, were carrying a very large crystal globe. It shimmered in the sunlight with a refractile pattern that was awe-inspiring. It was like a highly-detailed stained-glass orb yet every facet was a crystal-clear shape with beveled edges.

They flew it up to the medallion, carefully aligned it, then twisted it until it screwed into place. It was wild watching them spinning around in a synchronized flurry of rainbow-colored tornadic activity until it had been screwed in, nice and tight. Then they flew to the ground, landed, and turned to look up and watch it.

Kyrea's inner hopes began exploding with curious anticipation as Arlo stepped up beside her, his eyes, too, fixated on the sparkling globe as it shimmered with the pulse of a thousand stars.

For a long, breathless couple of moments, nothing seemed to happen. The air hung still, as though the world itself was holding its breath. But then, suddenly, the sky above Aeloria shimmered with blue hues warping into iridescent waves, as though the very fabric of the atmosphere was alive. The ground seemed to buzz, as if it, too, had been waiting for this magical moment.

A pulse of raw, ancient energy surged through the land, rippling out from the medallion and sending shockwaves of magic through the grass. The air thickened with power, and as the first rays of the midday sun touched the crystal sphere atop the totem pole, the earth seemed to tremble beneath Kyrea's feet. Light exploded from the globe in dazzling arcs, refracting into millions of rainbow prisms that shot across the land like beams of living color.

The prairie before her began to glow, like the embers of a fading fire. It grew in intensity until it pulsed with a vibrant radiance. The ground beneath her feet sent gentle shock-wave vibrations up her legs as if the earth itself was waking from an ancient slumber.

Kyrea watched with awe, her heart racing, as the first tendrils of green unfurled from the soil. The flowers began to grow at an incredible pace, so fast it almost seemed unreal. Like watching a timelapse video. Stems shot up like slender green arrows. Leaves sprouted in a rapid dance of life. Buds unfurled in bursts of color, revealing petals in every shape and color of the rainbow. Each bloom seemed to stretch toward the sun in living testament to the magic that had finally been returned to them.

Then the air grew suddenly warm with reborn energy, carrying with it the unmistakable scent of fresh, floral pollen. It was as if the land itself had become a living canvas, painted with strokes of magic and color that no mortal could have ever dreamed to see. The field had been transformed into a colorful paradise, a living, breathing land of light and color.

Kyrea's breath caught in her throat as she watched the flowers bloom and pulse with life. The petals of the flowers glistened as they unfolded, their colors deepening each second. Violet, pink, ruby, and gold, a living masterpiece in itself, shimmering in the sunlight. She had never seen anything so beautiful, so breathtaking. So full of pure magic and possibility.

"This... this is unbelievable," Kyrea whispered, her eyes wide as she watched the land transform before her eyes.

"This is only the beginning." The elder spoke with an excitement he could hardly contain.

She stood mesmerized, her heart filled with wonder as she took in the sight, overwhelmed by the beauty. Arlo, standing beside her, let out a low whistle of admiration. "Well, this is... something else," he muttered, his voice filled with awe.

And then, as if the flowers were aware of the power pulsing through the land, they began to release tiny, glittering particles into the air, magical pollen, like stardust drifting on the breeze, coating the air above the field like a glittery fog.

The fairies who had gathered around them watching, waiting, now shot out to the field in every direction. Each carrying various types of containers, buckets, baskets, jars and cups, anything they could find to gather the glittering pollen. With swift precision, they zipped around the sky in a whirlwind of activity and determined duty.

Kyrea watched as the fairies seemed to race against time to gather every bit of pollen before the wind blew it away. It seemed like mere minutes before the sun dipped down behind the trees and the light no longer illuminated the crystal globe. Once it did, Kyrea noticed the flowers sprouted no more glitter. What remained was all there was going to be… *for today?* She wondered.

The fairies, with containers full of sparkling pollen flew back to town. Kyrea let out a breath she hadn't realized she had been holding.

The elder fairy, his face now filled with peace, turned to her and rejoiced. "You've done it," he sang. "You've restored the heart of Aeloria."

Kyrea smiled, feeling a swell of satisfaction. Her heart pulsed with the knowledge that she had played a part in saving them. The fairies had their magic back, and Aeloria was alive once again.

That evening, the fairies celebrated the restoration of their magic with a grand feast. The fairy kingdom now glowed with a colorful bioluminescence she had only ever read about. Neon-like lights filled every crevice of town. Mushrooms glowed. Homes were well lit. Fairies shone like little bulbs of light. It was more beautiful than any picture or painting she had ever laid eyes on.

The elder held up an acorn goblet of fruit mead and declared loudly to the gathering of fairies. "In honor of Kyrea and Arlo, our two very special guests!" Cheering and joy erupted as everyone celebrated. Laughter and music filled the air as the glowing creatures danced in the twilight, their wings sparkling even in the night.

The tables were laden with fruits, pastries, and delicacies from the fairy land, and the sound of musical chimes, clinking glasses and merry chatter echoed through the warm night. As evening wore on, they sat around a glowing campfire, sharing stories of ancient magic and far-off lands.

As the firelight flickered and shadows stretched long into the night, some of the fairies began to drift off to bed. Arlo, exhausted from the day's excitement, curled up on a soft bed of moss that various fairies had made for him. He was soon asleep, his chest rising and falling in peaceful slumber. Many of the fairies who were still awake covered Arlo with flower petals, like a blanket.

But Kyrea, wide awake and full of energy, wandered through the fairy village, drawn to the quiet hum of the night. Some of the night-owl fairies were still busy with their crafts, tending to the gardens or weaving silken threads of magic, while others sat beneath the stars, their wings fluttering softly as they shared hushed conversations.

As she walked, a gentle voice reached her ears.

"Couldn't sleep?"

Kyrea turned and saw the elder fairy, his long white hair glowing faintly in the dim light.

"No," Kyrea said with a smile, still caught in the afterglow of the day's events. "That was the most beautiful sight I have ever seen!"

The elder's eyes sparkled with gratitude. "We owe you a great deal, Kyrea. Your kindness, your generosity, and your willingness to research the medallion and return it to us... We are forever in your debt. I wonder if there is something, anything, we could do to repay you for all you've done?"

Kyrea shook her head, a gentle laugh escaping her lips. "It's just what I do. I love going on adventures, exploring new places, solving puzzles, and discovering magical realms. It's what makes me happy. I don't need anything in return."

The elder studied her for a moment, his wise eyes filled with understanding. "You are quite the impressive young lady." He spoke with pride.

"Actually…" Kyrea paused and turned to him. "You may be the prefect fairy to ask – have you any idea what magical item or being could turn someone immortal, grant a wish or save a life?"

He looked at her curiously and with a thoughtful moment of pondering mentioned a few things that could possibly answer her question. "…though I've not heard of any of those items granting everlasting life. Immortality is a very special gift that can go two ways – either for good or can turn someone very, very bad. I am assuming we would be referring to someone who is quite good…" he trailed off with inquiry having suspected the magical presence of this girl was more than met the eyes.

"As far as I know I am good, though I have made mistakes in the past." She smiled coyly. "But when you don't age for a thousand years, you begin to suspect someone turned you immortal."

"I suspect you are right." The elder agreed and then continued, "there are so many worlds and realms, so many entities and creatures, so much magic and lore that exists now and has existed since the creation of life, I am sure you will have an extensive search before finding your answers."

"I believe you are right." She smiled as they kept walking along the pathway, side by side in silence. As they approached the elder's cottage, he stopped and turned to her again.

"Again, if you think of anything you want... or perhaps..." he paused thoughtfully, "...if your dragon friend would like something?"

Kyrea paused at the mention of Arlo. She glanced back at the sleeping dragon and sighed. The gears in her head began rotating as she thought of her friend's isolation and fear most of the time. "Well... I wouldn't dream of asking for anything myself, but..."

The elder leaned in slightly, curious. Kyrea hesitated, choosing her words carefully, then spoke from the heart. "Arlo... he's different from others. He's a dragon, quite possibly the last of his kind, at least in the realms I have visited. He feels very shy and vulnerable in public. When he's seen, people often react in fear. So, he doesn't like to draw attention to himself, and instead, he stays hidden in the shadows. I know it makes him feel isolated at times."

The elder nodded his understanding.

She took a deep breath before continuing. "If he had something, like a Paragon, something that could magically transform him into anything he desired, and then back to his true form, it would give him so much more freedom. He wouldn't feel like an outsider. He could go anywhere, do anything, without fear of being judged for what he is."

The elder's expression softened with empathy. He nodded thoughtfully. "Paragon." He paused on the word for a long, thoughtful moment. "Why, I haven't heard that word uttered from anyone's lips in at least seven generations..."

"I read about it in a fable, *oh my,* some four-hundred years ago, I believe. I found the premise, the idea fascinating, but at the time, couldn't imagine a use for such an item."

The elder nodded thoughtfully. "I understand," he said quietly. "To grant someone the freedom to be what they truly are, or even to choose something else entirely... it's a powerful gift."

Kyrea smiled gratefully, her heart light. "It could mean the world to him. And to me, too."

The elder's gaze lingered on Kyrea for a moment, and then he nodded once more. "Consider it done. We will see to it that a paragon is made for your friend with some of the magic we retrieved today. We would love to help his heart find peace."

Kyrea's eyes sparkled with gratitude. "Thank you. Oh thank you! I know he will love it and will always use it for good."

The elder smiled kindly, his wings fluttering softly as he turned to leave. "You are welcome, Kyrea. You have done much for us. Rest now, and know that you will always be an honorary friend to the Aelorian fairies."

As he disappeared into the night, Kyrea stood still for a moment, taking in the beauty of the glowing world around her. The stars twinkled brightly above, and the faint hum of magic in the air seemed to pulse in time with her heartbeat. She felt the weight of the day's adventures settle into a peaceful contentment.

Turning back to where Arlo lay, still asleep, she whispered softly, "Tomorrow will be a new day, my friend. A day full of endless possibilities."

The next morning, Kyrea woke to the sound of laughter in the air. She stretched, blinking away the remnants of sleep, and when she looked around, she saw many fairies were lined up, eagerly awaiting the noon-day sun, their eyes fixed on the horizon, ready for the next batch of flowers to bloom. Others were busy in their homes and labs, concocting various spells and magical creations. The air had a scent of enchanted herbs and shimmering dust.

"Kyrea!" Arlo sang as he swooped down to greet her, his voice filled with excitement. "Did you know that the princess's magical shoes were made from this flower pollen fairy dust that they collect here?"

"They were?" Kyrea eyes widened. She noticed that he was holding a bucket in his claws.

"Oh, yeah! Most of the magic in the world came from the fairies long ago," Arlo explained, his wings flapping with enthusiasm. "The reason there's so little magic left in the world these days is because the magical flowers stopped blooming. They thought all the power was lost forever. Can you believe that?"

Kyrea paused for a moment, taking in the weight of Arlo's words. "I had no idea," she said with a smile. It was incredible to think that so much of the magic she had encountered in her life, had ties to this little hidden world.

"I'm going to help the fairies collect pollen dust today. It seems like a grand time!"

They spent the next couple of days exploring, learning, and having fun. Arlo absorbed everything the fairies taught him; he enjoyed learning about how they craft the pollen dust into magical objects. He found the entire process fascinating.

The days passed in a blur of adventure and awe, but eventually, they both knew it was time to leave. As they prepared to depart, the elder fairy approached them, his face kind and wise as always. He handed Kyrea a small, delicate box, its surface glittered with a soft glow.

Kyrea looked at the box, then at the elder, her heart skipping a beat. "Is this…?"

The elder nodded shyly, then turned and walked away without another word.

Kyrea held the box against her chest for a moment smiling inside. She tucked it safely into her side bag, casting one last glance at the fairy village before finishing her goodbyes. The fairies waved and cheered them, gushing with thanks as they left.

Once outside the gates of Aeloria, Arlo turned to Kyrea, his face curious. "So… do you have any more of those 'Drink Me' bottles?"

Kyrea laughed softly, shaking her head. "Nope. I only got two. Besides, they're only good for shrinking someone down, not restoring them to original size."

"Oh," Arlo said, a little deflated. "Well, how do we get back to our regular sizes then?"

Kyrea grinned mischievously and reached into her side bag, pulling out a small container. She opened the lid with a flourish, revealing two slices of cake. "With this," she said, her eyes twinkling.

Arlo blinked at the cake in confusion. "Cake?" he asked, raising an eyebrow.

"Yes, cake," Kyrea winked with a nod, "I don't make up the rules, I just run with them." She handed the slice to Arlo, who without hesitation, took a bite. Within seconds, he shot up to his normal, towering size, his wings stretching wide as he looked around in surprise. Not wanting to waste any time, for fear Arlo may begin moving around and accidentally step on her, Kyrea quickly took a bite of her own slice, and in the blink of an eye, she was back to her regular size as well.

Arlo smiled brightly. "That was so much fun! Though I gotta admit, it's nice being back to my normal size again."

Kyrea chuckled, wiping crumbs from her lips. "Yeah, me too. It was fun in the fairy world, but there's something about being regular size."

Arlo gave her a playful nudge, his tail twitching in amusement. "Yeah, we've been to two places now where I felt small. I'd like to remain big for a bit."

Kyrea laughed, understanding exactly what he meant. It had been an adventure, one they would both treasure. But now, as they stood together in the open field once again, it looked completely different. Instead of tall tan grasses, it was a colorful field of wildflowers. Green plants with floral vines encapsulated the area like a magical forcefield. It was gorgeous. The world had been magically transformed, even though this was a small field, Kyrea had a feeling it would spread far and wide, eventually. Everything seemed a little bit bigger, a little more exciting, full of even more possibilities.

Kyrea looked to Arlo with an excited smile. "Where to next my friend?"

Arlo's eyes sparkling with the thrill of adventure. "I don't know, but I'm ready for anything. As long as there's food involved, I'm starving!"

WYVERSBANE

WOES

ARLO STRETCHED HIS WINGS and looked around. His stomach growled loudly, and he realized he had only eaten enough to keep a fairy alive. Scanning the surrounding prarie, feeling the pangs of hunger overtake him, his gaze landed upon some bushes with small, plump berries. Their deep, almost black, crimson hue stood out amongst the bright green leaves. They looked juicy and ripe; perfect for a quick snack.

Without a second thought, he wandered over and began picking berries, popping them into his mouth. The sweet, tangy flavor burst on his tongue, and he let out a satisfied sigh. He'd never seen berries like these before, but they certainly hit the spot.

Kyrea, sitting on a nearby stone, had pulled out her notebook and was flipping through its pages, looking for something. She wasn't hungry herself, so she absentmindedly kept reading. Her focus stayed on her task, as she immersed herself in her notes.

A minute later, Arlo walked over, a stem full of berries in his paw. He grinned at her and placed a small bunch of them on the open pages of her book.

"Want some?" he asked, speaking with his mouth full. His lips and tongue, stained dark purple from the berry juice, a sight that made her blink in surprise.

She glanced down at the berries, noting their strange shape and wicked dark color, but she was too distracted to say much at first. She looked up at Arlo, offering him a smiling, "No thanks." But as she spoke, a peculiar feeling stirred in her mind. A faint, almost imperceptible twinge of intuition. It was as if a quiet warning was being whispered to her, just out of reach, but enough to cause her a bit of unease.

She hesitated, staring at the berries for a moment longer. There was something about them that felt... *wrong.* She couldn't place it, but the more she looked at them, the more her mind churned with a vague sense of discomfort. Something in her soul recoiled, though she couldn't explain why.

Her fingers instinctively brushed against the leaves of the berries as she examined them closely, the familiar sensation of a long-lost memory flashing in her mind. She could almost recall reading about them—decades ago, maybe even centuries ago. It was like a distant shadow she couldn't quite catch, slipping through her thoughts just as she tried to focus on it.

"These berries haven't grown in ages," she murmured aloud, her mind still grappling with the growing sense of recognition. "I think they are connected to the fairy flowers... The fairy flowers only appear to us when we're small. But these... these berries are something different." She paused, trying to make the connection, but something about it unsettled her even more.

Why are they making me nervous? she thought.

She stood up, shaking off the unsettling feeling, and began to pace slowly. Something else tugged at her, a different memory. Without thinking, she opened a portal, her hand reaching inside it, searching for something she couldn't quite put into words. *Was it a book, or a scroll, or maybe a poem...* She wasn't sure.

Her hand sifted through the portal's depths, as if the magic itself knew what it was she was searching for. She could feel her thoughts aligning, and with a subtle shift, her fingers brushed against something wooden. She pulled it out and stared at it: a small, weathered placard, the type that might have once been posted along an old, forgotten trail.

Her eyes scanned the faded script, and as she read it, her heart skipped a beat.

Kyrea's blood ran cold as the realization hit her. The berries dangling from Arlo's claw, the ones he'd eaten, were *Wyversbane*—a plant cultivated through magic for a very specific purpose. She looked up at

Arlo, who was still oblivious to the danger, a satisfied grin on his face.

"Arlo, stop eating those!" she exclaimed, her voice sharp and urgent. She knocked the berry bunch from his hands and they tumbled to the ground.

Arlo blinked at her, confused, and then glanced down at the berries. "What's wrong? These are amazing!" he said, wiping berry juice from his mouth with the back of his paw.

Kyrea's mind raced, her thoughts a jumble of ancient texts and warnings she'd long forgotten. "*Wyversbane*," she whispered, feeling the weight of the word in the air between them. "Those berries are poison to dragons. They were magically created to eradicate the world of dragons."

Her heart hammered in her chest as she stared at the berries. She felt a sense of dread wash over her as she realized that Arlo was in serious danger.

Arlo's eyes widened, as a wave of realization passed over his face. He looked at the berries, then back to Kyrea. "Wait... You're telling me these berries are dangerous to dragons?"

She nodded, her mind spinning with the implications. "They're safe for humans, but to a dragon? They're deadly. These are *Wyversbane*— used long ago by wizards to keep dragons in check."

Arlo, still processing the news, gave a nervous laugh. "So, how many berries would it take to..."

Kyrea wasn't laughing. The name *Wyversbane* echoed in her mind, and with mounting dread, she opened another portal. This time, she pulled out a massive book, nearly the size of her torso. When she tried to open it, the weight caused it to fall from her hands and drop to the ground with a heavy thud. She collapsed to her knees, flipping through the pages frantically. She skimmed one paragraph, then grabbed a chunk of pages and flipped forward in haste, barely stopping long enough to read.

She was visibly frantic, her breath quickening as she scrambled through the pages. Arlo, watching her, could sense something was terribly wrong. His stomach twisted in unease.

Was it nerves, or... the berries?

Kyrea continued flipping through the pages, barely pausing to digest any of the words. She skimmed over a page, grabbed another handful of pages, and found it. The paragraph that mentioned *The Ballad of the Wyversbane Berries*. She frantically opened a portal while reaching into the book and withdrew a scroll. She unrolled it and read it aloud.

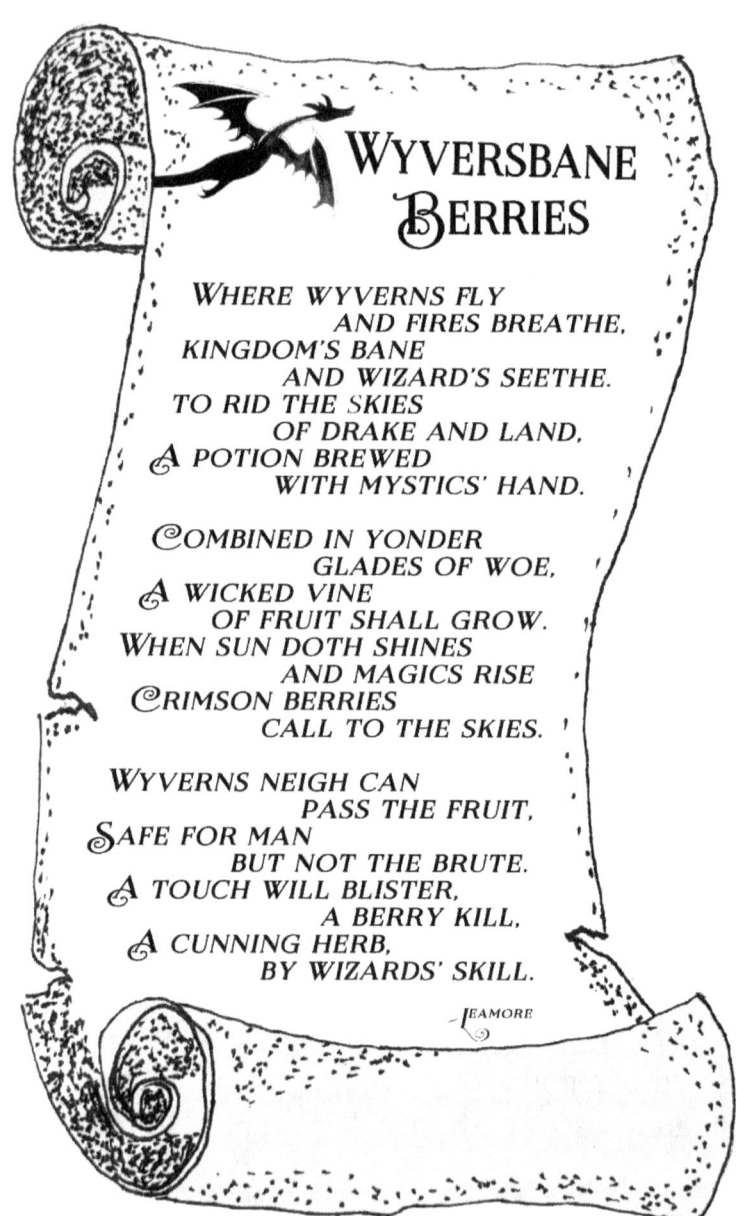

WYVERSBANE BERRIES

WHERE WYVERNS FLY
    AND FIRES BREATHE,
KINGDOM'S BANE
    AND WIZARD'S SEETHE.
TO RID THE SKIES
    OF DRAKE AND LAND,
A POTION BREWED
    WITH MYSTICS' HAND.

COMBINED IN YONDER
    GLADES OF WOE,
A WICKED VINE
    OF FRUIT SHALL GROW.
WHEN SUN DOTH SHINES
    AND MAGICS RISE
CRIMSON BERRIES
    CALL TO THE SKIES.

WYVERNS NEIGH CAN
    PASS THE FRUIT,
SAFE FOR MAN
    BUT NOT THE BRUTE.
A TOUCH WILL BLISTER,
    A BERRY KILL,
A CUNNING HERB,
    BY WIZARDS' SKILL.

TEAMORE

At the bottom of the scroll in a very faint fine print was the information she sought, the author. Squinting, attempting to make out the tiny words, she heard a low rumble.

"I don't feel so good..." Arlo mumbled weakly; his voice slurred. He was swaying on his feet, his balance faltering. He felt hot, his head pounding with a deafening pressure, and his vision began to spin. Nausea gripped his stomach as the world seemed to tilt beneath him.

He collapsed onto the ground, unconscious.

"Arlo!" Kyrea screamed, her heart lurching in panic. She rushed to his side. Her hand flew to his forehead, and the heat radiating from him nearly made her pull back. The color was draining from his scales, and his breathing had become shallow.

Her focus snapped back to the scroll. She reached into her side bag, found the magnifying glass and used to it to focus on the last word on the paper. Her eyes widened, not the author, the name of the town! Her mouth dropped open in shock. Dropping the scroll and glass, she jumped to her feet. There was no time to waste. Without a second thought, Kyrea bolted from the forest, her heart pounding as she sprinted west through the trees. She had to catch the last rays of sunlight before it was too late.

Kyrea ran faster than she had ever run before. The forest sped by in a blur. Branches reached out like claws, tearing at her clothes, snagging her hair, and cutting her skin as she powered through. The sharp sting of twigs and leaves lashing against her arms and face didn't slow her down. If anything, it spurred her on. Her mind focused only on one thing; getting to the clearing before it was too late.

As she neared the edge of the trees, Kyrea's fingers fumbled inside her side bag, desperate to find what she needed. She swirled her hand through the contents, feeling everything, until her fingers brushed against the familiar folded piece of paper. She yanked it out just as she burst into the clearing, the fading sunlight casting a warm, golden glow over the land.

Without hesitation, she held the paper up to the sky, the setting sun's rays illuminating the words written on it. Kyrea's voice rang out, urgent and steady, as she recited the incantation.

~ *When light shines through,*
~ *You'll see the way*
~ *Open brightly, on this day*
~ *A realm of wonders,*
~ *Await your word,*
~ *Speak, Bukas through the third.*

"Bukas, Bukas, Bukas!"

RETURN TO IEAMORE

A young ogre stood, scratching his head, staring at the strange object in front of him. It was like nothing he had ever seen before. A peculiar contraption with two wheels, handles, and what seemed to be some sort of seat, though it was much smaller than anything he'd ever seen.

The ogre had found it abandoned, laying on the ground near the outskirts of town. Curiosity had gotten the better of him, and he had spent the better part of an hour poking and prodding the odd object. *What could it be?* He had no idea.

With a grunt of curiosity, he turned the bicycle upside down, balancing it awkwardly on its handlebars and seat. He squinted down at the spinning wheels. "Hmm..." he muttered to himself, twisting his fingers through the wheel's spokes, making it spin faster.

It wasn't long before he noticed something peculiar. As the wheel turned, the chain attached to the gears *moved*. His eyes widened. He reached down to touch the chain, feeling the metal shift, and noticing how it made the wheels turn.

"Interesting," he mumbled, still uncertain of what exactly he was dealing with. He gave it another spin, fascinated by how the movement was so connected. *But what does it do?* he wondered, his mind struggling to put the pieces together.

He scratched his head again, then lifted the bicycle slightly, feeling the strange weight of it. His hands were too large, too clumsy, to really make sense of the thing. It wasn't a cart, or a wagon, or any sort of carriage he knew of. It was too small, too delicate for an ogre. He grunted in frustration, still perplexed. But then something happened.

A bright light flared up beside him, igniting the air like a spark in the dark. The ogre froze, his eyes widening in alarm as the light grew in intensity. He took a step back, his heart thudding in his chest. He had heard stories of strange magic, of portals and things appearing from out of nowhere, but he had never seen it for himself.

The light grew brighter, searing through the trees like a beacon. His instincts kicked in, and with a panicked yelp, the ogre dropped the bicycle to the ground and dashed behind the nearest tree. His large body squeezed behind the trunk, barely fitting as he crouched low, holding his breath.

He peered cautiously around the bark, his eyes wide with fear. *What could it be?* he thought, panic rising in his chest.

The young ogre watched from behind the tree as Kyrea leaped out from the light and took a look around at her surroundings. Spotting her bicycle lying before her was an answer to prayers. She ran to it, lifted it onto its tires and then leaped onto the seat, using the small peddles to advance her forward.

She raced off toward the town, her speed leaving the young ogre in awe. The way she had used the two-wheeled contraption, an object that had seemed so puzzling to him just moments before, was like watching a piece of magic in motion. He could barely comprehend the mechanics of it, but the way her legs moved, the way the wheels spun, it felt *alive*.

He thought about what it might mean if ogres could ride something like that. A machine like the bicycle could change everything for them! Faster travel, more freedom. But first, he had to figure out how to make it... *bigger.*

As Kyrea sped past the familiar landmarks of Ogre Town, she feared for Arlo's life. The wind whipped through her hair, her heart racing with the urgency of her mission. She could feel the weight of Arlo's life in every pedal stroke. She felt the panic in her chest as she neared the apothecary.

With a wild jump, she hopped off the bike mid-roll, sending it skidding to the ground as she sprinted into the apothecary store. The ogre inside, looking slightly gruff as an ogre would, acknowledged her entrance, his eyes glancing up in mild confusion.

"I need a dragon poison cure!" she blurted out, barely catching her breath. "NOW!"

The apothecary stared at her, his brows furrowing in perplexity. "A dragon?"

Kyrea nodded, still gasping to catch her breath, stopping just short of the counter. "Oh right, they were called Wyverns before. I've read the history." She could see the ogre's confusion. "I rescued a dragon, a Wyvern," she continued, her voice softening as her thoughts drifted to Arlo, "Actually, he saved himself. Arlo is my best friend, and he's been poisoned by Wyversbane." She paused, hoping the apothecary would understand. "Since dragons originated here in Ogre World, I thought you might be able to help me save him."

The apothecary studied her carefully, his gaze lingering on her as if trying to decipher her true intentions. His eyes softened, and after a long, awkward silence, he finally spoke. "I will help you, child. Wait here."

Without another word, he vanished into the depths of his store, leaving Kyrea to pace anxiously. She was far from an expert in ogre language, and even though she was trying to be patient, the seconds felt like hours. She caught sight of various bottles and jars lined on shelves, some of them labeled in ancient, flowing script so faint, she could barely read them.

Finally, after what felt like an eternity, the ogre emerged from the back room holding a dusty tome in his hand. His expression was grim but determined. He plopped the book down on the counter, blew off a cloud of dust and unlatched the lock. Kyrea watched as he opened the book, checked the table of contents and then flipped to the appropriate section.

His finger traced the lines, muttering to himself as he went. Kyrea couldn't read the ogre script, but she watched with deep attention, willing him to find what she needed. She watched him, glanced at the book, looked back up at him. Her adrenaline was racing but she knew her frantic emotions wouldn't help him study any faster.

She watched his fingers read the text, he pointed to a section and tapped it, "Yes, this is it!" He spoke happily, then turned the page, continuing to read.

She paced the room, waiting. The moments dragging on like days. She was just about to ask if there was anything else she could do when the apothecary broke the silence with a loud, "Aha!"

His bold declaration caused Kyrea to jump in surprise. She couldn't help the excitement that surged through her. "Did you find something?"

The apothecary glanced up. "I need leaves from a cinderlight plant, dragon-scourge root, and some vermillion extract. Go, gather them now."

Kyrea darted around the room, pulling the ingredients from the shelves as he continued to flip through the tome, muttering about ratios and preparation methods. Time felt like it was slipping away, but her heart raced as she placed each item carefully on the counter.

When the ogre finally returned from another room, he mixed the ingredients together, his deep voice murmuring instructions. He showed her the salve that had been created, "apply this paste to the blisters that would have developed from his touching or contacting Wyversbane."

But Kyrea's mind was already racing ahead. "I never saw any blisters. He ingested so many of the berries... and he went down so quick..." Her words kept trailing off as she was desperately trying to hold the emotions in. "He might not even be alive when I get back to him." Her words were strained, her voice trembling with fear.

The apothecary looked at her gravely, "no blisters..." his eyes returned to the book once more. "He *ate* the berries..." he shook his head sadly. He flipped through the pages again, muttering under his breath, and then... *aha*. His eyes lit up.

"I can make it work faster. But we need more ingredients, and we need something stronger."

Before Kyrea could ask what he meant, he was already in the back room again, pulling out a massive cauldron and additional supplies. The air around them crackled with urgency as he worked, his hands moving with expertise. He added a few gallons of Dracospire liquid into the concoction, his voice growing louder and more focused.

He then grabbed a large jug to pour it all into. "Can you lift this?" he asked, turning toward Kyrea with a skeptical look. This young girl was so small in stature... the jug was half her size.

"I will do whatever it takes to get this to Arlo!" She lifted it, but it was heavy. Really heavy. But she was immortal, she may not have excess strength, but she had willpower to see this through. "I will make it work. Now I just have to get back to my portal."

"*Back* to your portal?" The ogre asked.

She showed him the paper "All I need is sunlight and to recite this phrase and it should open up in the field next to the forest where Arlo went down." Kyrea was already fearing the journey.

"Forget sunlight," the ogre said as he pulled out a small clear ball from under the counter, "all you need is a sunflare orb, it will take you anywhere you want. Just think about where you want to be, use its light, say the phrase and simply jump through. It'll get you right to Arlo's side."

Kyrea could hardly contain her excitement. "That's *amazing*! You just saved me so much time!"

ARLO WAS SLIPPING AWAY, like the last embers of a dying fire. His breath was shallow, each inhale more labored than the last. Slowing with each passing second. The once-vibrant world around him was dimming into a haze of grey. The wind, which had been gently rustling the leaves earlier, had stilled. Even the bird songs that had filled the air with music went silent. He couldn't even hear the rhythm of his own heartbeats anymore.

The agony in his chest wasn't just physical. It was emotional. His best friend, Kyrea, the one person he thought would never abandon him, had left him.

She left me to die…

His mind drifted in and out of clarity. He thought of the old stories his ancestors had whispered to him as a hatchling. Dragon lore. Stories that were only ever passed down through dragons, and he was *the last*. A bitter taste of finality clung to his thoughts. If his lineage was truly gone, and Kyrea, had just... left? What was there for him to live for?

He couldn't take the sadness he felt when he regained consciousness after his fall, only to see Kyrea running away from him. He had no will, no energy to move, as he watched her running through the forest, away from him before he passed out again.

When he awoke a second time she was no longer in view. She had left him here. He was so confused, so hurt. His essence was draining, not just from the poison, but from the loss of everything that had ever mattered. A tear slid down his cheek.

He was ready to give up. Ready to succumb to the silence. If everyone was gone, everyone he ever loved, what was the point of holding on?

The light around him flickered; faint, as though even the sun was retreating in deference to his impending death. He closed his eyes, giving in.

Then, *crack*.

A blinding bolt of light split the air like lightning, and before he could comprehend what was happening, a figure appeared from the rift. It was Kyrea! She leapt through the portal like a rabbit, her body moving with frantic energy, clutching a large jug to her chest.

"Arlo, quick, drink this! Drink it all," she called, urgency lacing her voice.

His foggy mind struggled to process what was happening. He could barely focus. *Was this real? Or was it some fragment of his dying thoughts, a hallucination borne of desperate hope?*

Kyrea's face was flushed with exhaustion, her frazzled hair wild around her face, eyes wide with fear. She dropped to her knees beside him, her hands trembling as she lifted his head slightly. "Open your mouth! Drink this down." Her voice cracked with emotion. "You're going to have to help me out here. This jug is really heavy!"

A small amount of the liquid splashed into his mouth, and Arlo's senses recoiled from the taste. It was sour, sharp, almost rancid, and the smell was overwhelming; like rot mixed with herbs. Yet, it was real. The bitter reality of it forced him to awaken just enough to drink more. He lifted his head with what little strength remained.

Kyrea continued to pour the liquid into his mouth, her hands shaking as the jug wobbled in her grasp. He swallowed with desperate urgency, his body craving whatever it was that could save his life. Despite the awful taste, he felt the tiniest glimmer of hope. And then, within moments, something astonishing began to happen.

His heart, which had been slowing, painfully faltered, then stuttered, before it began to beat again, stronger, quicker. His muscles, which had felt like lead, began to respond. His vision cleared, the heavy fog lifting like mist in the morning sun.

"Take it easy," Kyrea's voice trembled with concern. "I don't know how quickly this works."

Arlo sat up, the ground beneath him feeling steadier now. "I think it's working already," he replied, his voice stronger. He flexed his claws, feeling the strength returning to his limbs.

Even as he healed, his eyes never left Kyrea.

She looked at him like he was the most precious thing in the world, her clothes torn, her eyes tired, her cheeks cut and red and clearly tear stained. Her expression was a chaotic mix of emotions: fear, hope, sadness, and a strong determination that he knew all too well. She cared.

She really cared.

Tears welled in Arlo's eyes, and he blinked rapidly, trying to push them back. It was the same feeling he had once had when he read that scene from the book about the pig and the spider. It was the kind of emotion that swells in your chest until you think you just might burst. He never thought he would feel that kind of vulnerability again, but here it was, stronger than ever.

With trembling paws, he pulled her into his chest. "You came back for me."

Her breath caught in her throat as she wrapped her arms around him, clutching him as if he might disappear. "Of course I came back for you. You're my best friend," she whispered fiercely. "I'd do anything for you. I'd go anywhere. I'd cross realms, fight trolls, outwit wizards, *anything,* to keep you safe."

Arlo held her tighter, feeling something inside him begin to stitch back together. "I thought you abandoned me," he whispered, his voice cracking with raw emotion. "I thought you left me. My heart... it felt so heavy. I think it was breaking."

Kyrea's throat tightened, a lump forming as she looked at Arlo. She hadn't even considered what her leaving had meant to him. To her, it had been an instinctive decision, to save him, to find a cure. But now, seeing the raw hurt in his eyes, the truth struck like a physical blow.

She had abandoned him.

In her fear and desperation, she'd acted without thinking about what her absence would cost, how it would feel to be left behind, alone, with the poison slowly draining his life. She'd been so focused on the cure, she'd never stopped to ask what it would mean for him to wake and find her gone.

The lump swelled in her throat. She swallowed hard, fighting the sting of tears. She could see it now, the confusion, the betrayal, the aching loneliness.

What had I done?

Her hands trembled as she brushed a tear from his brow, her fingers moving gently over his scales. He was healed now, yes. But the thought that he might have believed she'd left him to die... *that would haunt her.*

"I'm so sorry, Arlo," she whispered, voice thick with guilt. "I didn't even think about what you must have been feeling when I ran off. I... I just knew I needed to get the cure. I didn't mean to leave you. I promise. I thought... And you had passed out. To wait would've been... But I, I should've stayed. Right?"

She closed her eyes for a moment, taking in a shaky breath. She'd never been the kind of person to apologize easily, but the weight of this, what she had almost lost, helped her realize how much Arlo meant to her. *How much he always had.*

Arlo, though, just looked at her with a soft, understanding gaze. His claws gently cupped her face, and he shook his head slightly. "I know you did what you had to do. You were saving me. But I just... I didn't know if you would come back." He exhaled slowly; the air still heavy with feelings. "I thought I'd lost everything. Even you."

The words hit her heart like a blow, and she could barely hold back the rush of emotions threatening to burst. She had never realized how fragile their bond could have felt until that moment. She had thought of him as strong. He was a dragon. But she hadn't fully realized how much he needed her. *How much they needed each other.*

"You will NEVER lose me!" she vowed, her voice raw. "I swear it. You'll never be alone, not while I'm still breathing." She reached up, brushing a stray tear from his cheek, her touch tender.

Arlo's eyes softened, the pain in them slowly dissipating. He gave her a weak smile, though it was enough to melt the last remnants of the heaviness in her chest. "I fully expect us to separate for future adventures... just be sure to let me know where you are going and how long until your return."

The two of them sat there for a long moment, their bond stronger than ever, the unspoken understanding between them a silent promise. And though they both knew the road ahead would be fraught with more challenges, this moment, this raw, unguarded exchange, reminded them that as long as they had each other, they could face anything.

Even the impossible.

ᴄᴛʜᴇ ᴅʜɪsᴛᴏʀʏ ᴏғ Wʏᴠᴇʀs

Over the course of the next few days, Kyrea refused to leave Arlo's side. She had to take some time to piece together the puzzle for Arlo. How did she know what caused his illness? How did she know the ogres would have a cure for him? The history lesson behind it all… was a powerful shock.

"According to a manuscript I read long before we met, Ogres and dragons once shared a realm together. It should come as no shock the fact that you have so many similarities with ogres." Kyrea began carefully, so as to lighten the message.

Arlo scoffed as he remembered the smell that wafted from the ogre town. "Preposterous!"

"You both are large, enormous when compared to humans. You are both strong, powerful beings, physically dominant with protective abilities." Kyrea quickly rattled off some facts. "Territorial. Known to be hoarders especially of what's foreseen as treasure. Your lives are extended, living life spans so long you could almost befall as immortal, at least when it comes to age. Both resistant to most magics."

Arlo rolled his fingers with a look of; go on, finish your story, though Kyrea could tell he did not like being compared to ogres.

"Back then, dragons and ogres were very close to each other, like dogs are to humans. More than mere pets, they were companions. So, when a bunch of dragons began dying of some strange illness the ogre apothecaries of the realm gathered to figure out what was taking the lives of their precious friends."

Arlo was still trying to comprehend that his ancestors originated in towns like Leamore, but he kept listening to Kyrea's story.

"Apparently it all came down to that wacky plant that bloomed the Wyversbane berries. While the plant was harmless to ogres, the leaves, the stems, even the flowers if they touched a dragon's skin it would cause blisters. But worse, there was a liquid within the berries designed to kill dragons."

"The plant was called Wyversbane?" Arlo inquired. "Where did that name come from?"

"The ogres named it. They named it Wyver, which is what they used to call dragons, and bane, which means cause of great distress. And this plant truly DID distress them. They cut down and killed every plant in the realm, burned it to ash and then dumped the ash in the ocean. They thought they had eradicated it but it kept coming back, like a weed. They created potions to kill it, poisons of all sorts and when it kept returning, they researched its origins and followed the timeline to Medieval Times."

"The Knights?!" Arlo's eyes widened.

"They decided to kill it in its initial conception, by eradicating the botanist that designed it. If it were never created the dragons never would have died."

Arlo was on the edge of his tail.

"They turned to an ancient form of time travel known by the elders, called Temporae."

"Ogres can travel through time?" Arlo sat up curiously. *How had he never heard this?*

Kyrea cocked her head to the side. "They used to." She didn't feel it right to jump ahead in the story.

When Arlo had settled back down, she continued. "They opened a portal and sent some of their best ogres back to solve this problem. But... unfortunately, a couple of dragons went through with them. The dragons thought the realm was beautiful and it smelled..."

"Fabulous." Arlo finished her thought with a dreamy look. Then the reality occurred to him: That's exactly why the dragons left, they realized there were places that smelled better than ogre world.

Kyrea glanced at him, reading his thoughts. She pursed her lips together and shrunk down as she sat. "You're right. They decided to stay. And it broke the ogre's hearts."

Arlo's mouth dropped open. He thought about it for a long pause, Kyrea waiting until he understood.

"So…" he began shyly, "dragon's chose to leave the world they were meant for, and leave the ogres that loved them and considered them companions. All while the ogres were doing this to rid the world of a plant designed to kill dragons…" Kyrea nodded as he spoke. He slowly continued, "And they stayed in the human realm, in the past, only to be eradicated by the humans of the land." Arlo's stomach churned. "We're extinct because of our choices."

"Your extinct because the ogres chose not to kill the botanist, the wizard, but to kill the plants he was creating." Kyrea tried to soften the blow but as soon as the word *extinct* exited her mouth she regretted it. She could see him twinge at hearing that word in her voice. She hated the idea of hurting him, "But Arlo," she hesitated, "it gets worse."

"How could it get any worse?!?" Arlo nearly screeched. Kyrea could tell this was hitting him hard.

"Because, they arrived in the time before the plant was created." Kyrea spoke softly. "It was created to kill the enormously large and frightening dragons that showed up out of nowhere and began burning their fields and eating their livestock. They were trying to get rid of a pest."

Arlo's eyes became blank; there was suddenly no spark. His facial expression became hollow. He sat there with a distant gaze, emotionless. He looked detached. Pale. As if he were only a shell of a dragon.

Kyrea's heart burst for him. She knew this was a horrible story, but history is often harsh and unsettling. She gave him time, to see if he would come back to her on his own, and after a little while, he did. As a single tear slipped down his scaly cheek, she spoke again, with extreme care.

"The ogres didn't want to lose the Wyvers, but they didn't want to hold them back, either. They gave them their freedom. But they never gave up on the dragons. They developed a cure for the berries. They published it in every realm, so anyone would know how to treat a poisoned dragon. I read about it a long, long time ago, but came across a short story from a book in the Giant's library just recently."

Arlo looked down at Kyrea with a faint smile.

"I didn't know if it was true, but when you collapsed, when I realized what you had eaten, and recognized the plant, I held onto hope that the story *was* true, so I could save your life.... And it was."

After some contemplative time with his thoughts Arlo had to ask one more question. The berries had been eradicated from time... they weren't here when we arrived to visit fairy world, and you said, they returned...

Kyrea grimaced, the look in her eyes was full of sadness and regret and a little conflict. "I think it is because we restored magic to the area."

Arlo kept the rest of his thoughts to himself. If he truly were the last dragon, he just needed to remember these berries and stay away from them.

But there was a lot more cycling through his thoughts than just that. He had survived a near-death experience and he needed time to make sense of what he had been through.

Kyrea awoke under the sprawling branches of an ancient oak tree. Its limbs stretched out in every direction, creating a dance of shifting shadows and dappled light on the earth beneath her. She squinted up at the sky, but the sunlight filtering through the leaves made it hard to tell what time of day it was.

As she slowly sat up, something startled her. She didn't recognize where she was. She frowned, her heart skipping a beat, but then she noticed something comforting—her favorite book was lying open on her chest. The pages fluttered as she moved. She picked it up, glancing at the open pages, and noted where a delicate ribbon marked the spot where she'd left off. She closed it carefully, a little puzzled by her surroundings.

Before she could think on it too much, a rustling sound broke through her thoughts. The dog, who had been lying next to her, stirred awake. Arlo, her ever-loyal companion, stretched his front legs out in a grand, sleepy arch before turning toward her with a soft woof. He leaned in and kissed her cheek, his cool wet nose tickling her skin.

Kyrea laughed softly, wiping her face. "Oh, Arlo. What a beautiful day it is!" she said, ruffling his soft, golden fur.

Arlo's tail wagged furiously, his whole-body wiggling with excitement. His bright eyes sparkled with the kind of pure joy only a dog could have. Kyrea grinned and pushed herself to her feet, stretching her arms above her head.

"What do you want to do now?" she asked, looking down at him. He was looking up at her with those adoring brown puppy dog eyes.

Without missing a beat, Arlo trotted off to the other side of the oak tree. She watched curiously as he disappeared behind the thick trunk, only to emerge on the other side seconds later with a large, weathered stick clutched in his mouth. He presented it to her, his tail wagging even faster.

"Fetch! What a great idea!" Kyrea exclaimed, her eyes lighting up. She reached down, took the stick from his mouth and tossed it as far as she could across the meadow. Arlo shot off like a streak of gold, his paws pounding the soft earth as he raced to catch it.

The game went on for what felt like hours. Arlo never seemed to tire, fetching the stick again and again, his energy boundless. Eventually, though, he flopped down on the ground, panting, and began gnawing on the stick. Kyrea sat down next to him, leaning back against the sturdy oak tree. She looked up at the sky, still unsure of where she was, but feeling an overwhelming sense of peace.

The soft thrum of wind in the leaves reminded her of her book, still resting beside her. She reached for it, the familiar cover offering her comfort, and opened it to the page she had left off on. As she settled back into the story, her mind wandered again… *was this real? Or was it part of a dream?*

The thought was fleeting, and soon the world of the book swallowed her up once more.

Kyrea woke with a start.

Her eyes flew open, and for a moment, she was disoriented, unsure of where she was. The familiar hum of morning filled the air; birds chirping, the soft rustle of leaves, the cool breeze against her skin. It felt like the dream had followed her into the waking world. She stretched her arms high above her head and took a deep breath, her body aching with the usual remnants of sleep.

What an odd dream, she thought to herself. *It was me, and there was a dog. And I called him Arlo?*

Just as she tried to shake off the confusion, she felt a familiar nudge against her leg. Arlo—the dragon—his tail had been swishing like a rattlesnake as he slept. But when he heard her say his name he slowly pulled from his slumber and opened his eyes.

"You called for me?" he asked, his head tilting in a familiar, endearing way.

Kyrea blinked, momentarily thrown off balance by the strange thought. "Oh! I'm sorry. I was just thinking about the dream I just had."

Arlo gave a soft, lazy hmmm, as though he'd been half-listening. Then with a rapid flip of emotion, he perked up excitedly. "Oh, I had an interesting dream, too! Let me tell you about it," he said, his tail swishing behind him as he sat up beside her.

Kyrea smiled, "Alright, Arlo, let's hear it then. What was your dream about?"

Arlo gave a soft sigh, his eyes closing for a moment as he gathered his thoughts. "Well, it was about... you. But you were a fish and you were blowing bubbles underwater."

Kyrea laughed, quickly forgetting her dream. This was much more fun to listen to.

PARAGON

POSSIBILITIES

ΑS THE SUN ROSE, CASTING LONG pink streaks across the sky Arlo woke up with determination, "Let's get out of here."

Kyrea, still sleeping, opened her eyes with a smile. With a graceful stretch, she gathered her things and climbed onto Arlo's back. Without a word, Arlo spread his wings wide and shot into the air, his powerful muscles propelling them upwards. The air was crisp, cool with the morning dew, and the winds swirled around them as they climbed higher.

They soared over lush forests, glittering rivers, and snow-capped peaks, the world unfolding beneath them. The horizon stretched out, endless, an open invitation to whatever lay beyond. Hours passed, the world beneath them slowly changing as they ventured farther from the familiar, without any specific destination in mind.

Finally, after what seemed like an eternity of flight, the sight of something vast and endless caught Arlo's eye. He veered slightly to the right, heading toward a large body of water; the ocean. They flew over the shimmering beach and out across the waters, the salt of the sea and the call of the distant gulls filling the air. The colors of the ocean were brilliant, the waves sparkling like diamonds under the sun.

Arlo pressed onward, until they came upon a tiny, secluded island. Barely more than a few rocky outcrops surrounded by smooth, white sand, it was far too small to support any human life. That was a perfect place in Arlo's mind. His wings beat slowly as he descended, the weight of his body and wings sending a ripple through the ocean below. He landed with ease, his claws sinking slightly into the sand.

They sat on the shore, watching as the waves rolled in, the rhythmic sound of the ocean filling the air. The horizon stretched out before them, beautiful and vast, and yet Arlo felt an odd stirring deep inside him. His golden eyes traced the endless expanse of blue and green, but something was missing.

"What's wrong?" Kyrea asked, breaking the silence. She glanced at him, "You don't want to explore? Swim with dolphins, explore the coral reefs?"

Arlo's gaze lingered on the ocean, and with a deep breath, he gave a firm shake of his head. "No," he said, his voice steady and resolute. "Water will put out dragon fire. I don't want to get anywhere near it."

Kyrea's face fell slightly, but then a spark of excitement lit up her eyes. "Oh!" she jumped to her feet so suddenly, it was as if she had been bitten by ants. "I forgot! I can't believe I forgot! During all the emotional turbulence of the past couple days, I completely forgot about the gift I got you!"

Arlo blinked his large golden eyes. "You got ME a gift?" A smile spread across his face.

She nodded, grinning as she reached into her side bag and pulled out a small, sparkly box. "I had the fairies make this for you," she said, holding the box in her palm stretched out to him.

He stared at the box, intrigued but puzzled. It was delicate, shimmering with hints of light. He sniffed it, the soft scent of wisteria and fresh flower pollen tickling his nostrils. "What is it?" he took the box into his claws and stared at it, bringing it right up to his eye to inspect further.

"Open it!" Kyrea urged; her voice filled with an excited anticipation she could hardly contain. She couldn't wait to see it herself.

Arlo opened the box slowly, revealing a small, golden pendant. It shimmered in the sunlight, the shape of a paw print glowing with an inner magic. He looked at it, perplexed. "Again, I ask, what is this?"

Kyrea smiled, her eyes lighting up as she watched him examine the pendant. "This is a very special, one-of-a-kind gift. I had the fairies make it for you. It's called a Paragon."

"A paragon?" Arlo repeated, the word which was unfamiliar in his mind.

She was eager to see it and Arlo could tell. He lowered the box so she could look inside. Once she was able to see the pendant she rephrased, "Actually, I guess we could call it a Paragon Paw. A paragon is a very special, very rare magical item capable of great things. What I requested is something that would allow you to change into anything you want to become, until you choose to change back to yourself."

"To change?" Arlo asked, uncertain. The idea didn't sit comfortably with him, but Kyrea continued.

"You will always be a dragon," she explained, her voice gentle but full of enthusiasm. "But with this particular paragon, you *should* be able to transform yourself into any other living creature in the world. This way, you can go anywhere you want without fearing humans as you would as a dragon."

Arlo cocked his head, a hint of skepticism in his eyes. "Transform? Transform how?"

Kyrea reached into the box and pulled out a small piece of folded paper. She unfolded it, and noticed it was a poem which contained instructions intricately crafted from the fairies. She read it aloud as it contained the instructions on how to use the Paragon Paw.

A Paragon will heed your plea,
And grant you what your mind might see.
To use this charm just tap it thrice.
And wish for what your heart thinks twice.
Place it safe. And know it's true.
The Paragon is here for you.
A gift of magic, light, and grace.
A token sweet for dreams to chase.

She handed it to Arlo, her hands trembling with excitement. "So how this works, Arlo, is you'll want to first place it somewhere really, really, really safe. Someplace no one can see or get to. Ever!"

"Like under my protective armored scales near my heart chamber?" Arlo asked, his gaze thoughtful.

"Exactly," Kyrea nodded enthusiastically. "Then, according to the ballad, you think the magic words, tap your chest three times fast, and then think about what you want to become. You'll immediately change into that creature and gain all of its abilities."

Arlo looked at the pendant for a long moment, unsure whether he liked the idea or not. But when he glanced up and saw seagulls soaring overhead, a thought sparked. "So, if I wanted to turn into a seagull… all I would have to do is tap my chest and think about it?"

Kyrea smiled, nodding. "From what I understand, yes. Want to give it a try?"

Arlo stood there for a moment, contemplating. He placed the Paragon Paw safely beneath his armored scales and, after a deep breath, closed his eyes. He thought about the seagulls above, their wings spreading wide, soaring gracefully in the open sky.

He tapped his chest three times quick.

In an instant, with a soft, magical poof, Arlo transformed. He stood before Kyrea, now in the form of a seagull. He looked up at her in confusion, his sharp beak and eyes now tiny compared to his usual dragon self. "Did it work?" He asked.

Kyrea giggled, her laughter like music. "Why don't you flap your wings and find out?" she suggested, her voice full of amusement.

Arlo hesitated but then gave his wings a tentative flap. To his surprise, he took off into the air, his wings beating more often than when he was a dragon. He could feel the feathers on his wings, tickling him as the wind rustled through them. He saw the tiny shadow of a seagull on the sand beneath him. He flew down and landed next to her. "Can I see myself? Do you have a mirror?"

Kyrea opened her side bag and pulled out a small mirror compact. She opened it, revealing the reflection of Arlo, now in seagull form. "Wow! I'm a seagull. I can't believe this."

Then, panic hit him. "Wait a second, I'm a dragon! I should be a dragon! This is horrible! How do I become a dragon again?"

Kyrea's voice was reassuring. "Calm down, Arlo. Just think about yourself as a dragon and then tap your chest with your wing."

His heart was pounding, but he tried to slow his breathing. With a deep breath, he closed his eyes and tapped his chest once more, focusing on the form he was most familiar with, the mighty dragon.

With another soft poof, he was back, towering over Kyrea once again, his green scales gleaming in the sunlight. He turned and looked at himself and smiled with a deep exhale. *Whew!*

Arlo inspected himself in the compact mirror's reflection. "Oh, thank goodness. That scared me."

Kyrea smiled warmly. "What do you think, Arlo? Do you like the gift?"

Arlo paused, his mind racing. He had never considered becoming anything else but a dragon. It felt strange, yet freeing. He thought back to the dangers he had faced recently, being the last dragon.

But now, with this gift, he didn't have to hide anymore. He didn't have to be ashamed.

He looked at Kyrea, the girl who had always seen him for what he truly was, and nodded. "Yes. I do think I like it. Thank you, Kyrea."

Arlo was deep in thought when a small crab scurried out of the ocean waves and across the sand. Its sideways walk, with those big pincers clacking rhythmically, caught his attention. The little creature seemed to wear a permanent scowl on its face as it marched past, entirely focused on its journey. Arlo couldn't help but laugh at it, a low rumble echoing from his chest.

Kyrea glanced up at him, curious about his sudden amusement. "What's so funny?"

"Look at it," Arlo said, gesturing with a wing toward the crab. "The way it walks… sideways... and the angry look on its face!" He chuckled again, a playful spark in his golden eyes.

"I'm going to try it," Arlo announced, tapping his chest with his paw. The magic of the Paragon surged through him, and in an instant, he shrunk down into the form of a crab. The weight of his body shifted, and he found himself awkwardly balancing on his tiny legs.

He tried to walk forward, but, of course, he couldn't. His body insisted on moving sideways with each step, in the same manner as the crab. With each sideways shuffle, Arlo couldn't help but let out a hoot of laughter. It was a strange, unique experience.

"Okay, okay, this is not how I thought walking like a crab would feel!" Arlo called out, his voice muffled and high-pitched in the crab form.

After a minute of awkward sideways shuffling, he tapped his chest again, and with a poof, returned to his dragon form. He stretched his wings and let out a relieved sigh, his body feeling much more at ease in his original shape.

Kyrea had been sitting on the beach, watching the whole spectacle with a bemused smile. She raised an eyebrow at him. "How was it, Arlo?"

Arlo puffed out a breath, his wings fluttering in an attempt to shake off the strange sensation. "I've got to say, I don't think I'm cut out for crab life."

Kyrea laughed, "I don't think anyone's cut out for crab life... including the crab."

But just as they both relaxed, Arlo's sharp eyes caught a new sight, a hermit crab. Its oversized shell wobbling on its back as it scuttled across the sand had his curiosity piqued. Arlo couldn't resist.

He tapped his chest again, and poof—he was a hermit crab. At first, the sensation of carrying the heavy shell was strange, almost oppressive. The weight was overwhelming, as though he had the weight of the world on his back. He moved, trying to walk like he imagined a hermit crab would, but found himself toppling sideways. He hadn't realized that he needed to hold on to the shell. The shell rolled off, leaving him exposed and vulnerable.

Arlo's tiny hermit crab body froze in panic as the feeling of being "naked" swept over him. He quickly tapped his chest, and with another poof, was back to his dragon form.

He picked up the shell gingerly with one of his claws, peering inside with one golden eye. A low humph escaped his throat as he realized he wasn't quite built for this either. "That wasn't so great."

Kyrea looked up from her notebook and smiled at him, her expression warm. "You do seem to have a knack for picking creatures with... *challenges.*"

Arlo glanced over at the ocean again and noticed a sea turtle slowly pulling herself onto the shore. She moved with purpose, her flippers scraping through the sand as she made her way toward a spot to lay her eggs. The quiet focus of her movement intrigued him. The dragon's curiosity bubbled up once more. "I wonder what it feels like to be a sea turtle," Arlo muttered to himself. He tapped his chest, and poof, he was a sea turtle.

Immediately, he felt the weight of the shell again. The difference was even more dramatic now. The shell felt like an immovable weight, and moving it felt as though he were dragging a mountain on top of him. Arlo tried to push forward, but his flippers could hardly pull him forward. He didn't like it one bit. However, when he tried to reach under the shell to turn back, he found that he couldn't! He struggled, flailing awkwardly, he was kicking up sand all over the place as he panicked.

"Kyrea!" he called out in frustration, his voice muffled. "I can't reach my chest!"

Kyrea, who had been observing from a distance, jumped up and rushed to his side. She knelt down, lifting one side of Arlo's turtle body, giving him enough room to push his flipper under the weight of the shell. With a grunt, Arlo was able to tap his chest, and poof, he was a dragon again.

His large dragon body was suddenly free of the heavy shell, but the force of his transformation sent a wave of sand flying in all directions. His giant form loomed over Kyrea, and the sudden change knocked her onto her back with a soft thud. She looked up at him, leaning back on her elbows, and smiled.

"Are you okay?" she asked, her voice full of concern and a slight amusement.

Arlo exhaled a sharp breath, shaking his head. "I couldn't reach my chest! I couldn't turn back! If you weren't here, I would have been stuck that way! Oh, I don't like this at all. No, no, no!"

Kyrea chuckled, brushing sand off her clothes as she sat up. "I'm sorry, Arlo. I really thought you'd enjoy it. But of course, you picked a creature which doesn't spend much time on land. Sea turtles only come ashore to lay their eggs. Male sea turtles never leave the water."

Arlo blinked, then groaned in frustration. "I can't believe I didn't think of that."

Kyrea grinned and gave him a teasing look. "What about the water? Maybe being a sea turtle in the ocean would be different."

Arlo gave her a sideways glance, eyeing the waves. "But what about my dragon fire?" he asked, nervous at the thought. "If I'm a sea turtle in the water and I change back into a dragon, I'll be underwater, and my fire would be extinguished! No, no, no. This is not a good idea."

Kyrea waved a hand dismissively. "You don't have to change from a sea turtle to a dragon. You could become a crab instead, walk out of the water, and THEN turn back into a dragon."

Arlo stopped, his mind racing. A crab. He could be a crab and then walk away from the water. His mind swirled with possibilities, and he turned toward the small crab he had seen earlier. A flock of sea gulls were circling above him. Arlo realized the crab was seconds from becoming their dinner. With a tap of his chest, Arlo *poofed* into a seagull and flew around angrily, chasing them away from the crab. When the crab was safe, he landed back by Kyrea.

"Not good. If I am small like a crab, I am vulnerable to predators."

"So, think big." Kyrea smiled. "Become a very large crab that no one would want to tangle with."

A glint of mischief sparkled in his eyes. He looked over at the crab, and with a deep breath, he tapped his chest once more and thought *big*. He visualized himself as a giant crab, roughly Kyrea's size, strong and formidable.

Poof.

A massive crab, easily ten feet tall, appeared before Kyrea. The ground beneath his massive claws rumbled slightly as the giant pincers clicked together. He looked down at Kyrea, who had jumped back a few steps, wide-eyed.

She blinked, speechless for a moment, before breaking into a laugh. "Arlo! You're HUGE!"

He looked down at his giant claws, flexing them experimentally. He realized how imposing he must look. "I *did* think big," Arlo said with a chuckle, his crabby voice deep and amused.

Kyrea smiled and nodded. "Well, there's your answer. Now you can be any size you want to be, so long as you just imagine it."

Arlo tapped his chest again and turned back into his dragon form, still standing tall above Kyrea. "Now *that* is intriguing," he mused, a thoughtful expression crossing his face. "Let me think about this some more." He sat down to contemplate his newfound opportunities.

As Arlo paced the beach, deep in thought, Kyrea returned to her notebook, but she couldn't help but glance up every once in a while. She watched with a grin as Arlo changed form again and again, experimenting with creatures both big and small. He turned into a horse, standing tall on four hooves, his mane billowing in the breeze. Then, a hunting dog, barking and scaring a flock of seagulls into the sky.

Kyrea giggled at the sight of him chasing after the birds, then returned to her notes, content to allow her friend explore the wonders of his new gift.

A few minutes later, the midday sun was blocked by an enormous shadow. Kyrea looked up to see Arlo standing over her. "Can I help you?"

Arlo's eyes gleamed with excitement. "I want to go into the ocean. I want to go into the ocean and explore it!"

"Okay, Arlo. Go ahead."

"I want to talk to you about it first," he said, pacing around her. "I don't want to take any chances with my dragon fire."

She nodded thoughtfully. "Okay, should we put together a plan?"

"Yes! I like plans," Arlo agreed eagerly, sitting down beside her.

They began discussing their options: the creatures and wonders of the ocean that Arlo could turn into, considering the best ones with the ability to tap his chest.

"Oh, yes, I think whales are amazing," Arlo mused, his eyes lighting up. "And people can fit inside of them and shoot out from their blowholes! I could totally try that!"

Kyrea chuckled, shaking her head. "Well, yes, I do remember that story too. But I'm not sure how accurate it is. I mean, it sounds fun, but..."

Arlo grinned. "Imagine that! I could just… shoot you out of a whale's blowhole! What else is out there in the ocean?"

He paused for a moment before his eyes widened with a new thought. "What about a submarine? Can I turn into a submarine?"

Kyrea's brow furrowed as she considered it. "That's a tricky one. A submarine is man-made, and it's not a living creature. So I'm not sure the paragon can do it. Plus, if you can't move, you can't touch your chest to turn back into a dragon. It's a no-go, I do believe," Kyrea concluded.

Arlo's wings drooped slightly. "Oh, right… I didn't want to be a submarine anyway."

Kyrea smiled and nodded. "I think it's for the best. But hey, there are plenty of other sea creatures."

Arlo's curiosity didn't stop there, though. He tilted his head, thinking deeply. "Could I become a tree or a flower? They're alive…"

Kyrea grinned at him. "Well, yes, they're alive, but trees don't really move, do they? I've heard of magical trees that can walk, there's this one kind called the walking palm trees that supposedly move so slowly you can't even see it, but with your magic, maybe you could become one of those. Still, I think you might want to stick to something that moves quicker, like animals."

Arlo shuddered. "No, no, I don't want to be a tree for the rest of my life!"

Kyrea laughed, placing a reassuring hand on his large, scaly arm. "Don't worry, Arlo. As long as I'm around, I'll help you turn back. You'll never stay a tree for long." She winked. "But yeah, animals are probably your best bet. There are so many amazing creatures in the ocean!"

"I've read about octopus," Arlo continued, his eyes lighting up. "And dolphins! They're so smart! But what about fish? I think they're kind of fun, too. But fish get eaten. I don't want to be eaten."

Kyrea's smile remained, warm. "Remember, if you're ever in danger, you can just touch your chest and turn into something bigger, bigger than what's chasing you."

Arlo's face lit up with the idea. "Maybe... maybe I should become a predator!"

Kyrea raised an eyebrow. "Like what?"

Arlo thought for a moment, then his grin grew wide. "A shark! A great white shark! They're huge and humans are terrified of them!"

Kyrea chuckled. "Yes, they are. But sharks aren't invincible. They have their own predators in the ocean. If a fishing vessel catches you with a net, you'd be stuck. But if that happened, you could shrink into a tiny fish and slip through the holes!"

Arlo blinked, fascinated. "So I could go from one animal to another without needing to change back into a dragon?"

"Exactly," Kyrea nodded. "Want to try it?"

Arlo's eyes gleamed with the challenge. "Sure! Let's see what I can do."

Kyrea grinned. "Okay, let's start simple. First, change into a monkey."

"A monkey?" Arlo echoed, cocking his head.

"Yes, then a parrot, then a lion... and then how about a frog?"

Arlo laughed at the idea. "Alright! Monkey, parrot, lion... and frog! This will be fun."

He closed his eyes, took a deep breath, and with a poof, transformed into a small, playful monkey with long slender tail. He hopped up a nearby tree and swung from branch to branch, chattering as he did. His tail wrapped around a branch, and he hung there for a moment, before tapping his chest. *Poof!* He was a parrot, soaring high into the sky with brilliant red, yellow, and blue feathers.

He flew through the air, but, as he neared the ground, he tapped his chest again. *Poof!* He became a lion, his powerful roar echoing across the beach.

Kyrea, still smiling, watched with amusement as Arlo demonstrated his ability to switch seamlessly between forms. He then tapped his chest and shrunk down to the size of a frog. He hopped toward Kyrea, ribbiting in his tiny voice.

Kyrea bent down and cupped the frog gently in her hands, bringing him close to her face. She smiled and kissed him softly on the top of his head, a playful gesture. When she set him down, Arlo tapped his chest again, returning to his dragon form.

"Why did you kiss me?" he asked.

Kyrea giggled, her eyes twinkled with mischief. "I thought you might turn into a prince! You know, from the story?"

Arlo's eyes widened in mock horror. "You wanted to see if I'd become a human?"

Kyrea nodded, laughing. "I think you should stick with animals for now, though. Master those first, and then we can talk about humans."

Arlo thought about this, his dragon head tilting in contemplation. He didn't answer right away, lost in his own thoughts.

After a long moment, Kyrea returned to her notebook, flipping through the pages quietly as Arlo stared out at the ocean. Time seemed to stretch on, and then, without another word, Arlo turned around and tapped his chest again.

Poof!

He transformed into a pelican, soaring up into the sky, his wings catching the breeze. Kyrea looked up as he circled around the water, diving close to the surface. She watched in awe as Arlo's beak opened, catching a few fish from the ocean before flying back to the beach. He landed gracefully next to her, opened his mouth, and dropped the fish onto the sand.

With a proud smile, Arlo tapped his chest once more and poofed back into his dragon form.

"I think we should gather some firewood and cook our dinner," Arlo said, his tone more serious now but still excited from his adventures.

Kyrea smiled warmly. "I think that's an excellent idea, my friend."

They spent the rest of the evening discussing all the creatures of the ocean, as they planned for Arlo's Ocean Adventure. Tomorrow, he would dive into the depths of a world he'd only ever read about. His heart was full of anticipation. The excitement of exploring new worlds fueled his every thought.

And, for Arlo, *this was only the beginning.*

THE END... *for now.*

COMING UP

IN THIS SERIES:

THE IMMORTAL EXPLORER, CHASING REFLECTIONS 2

Mirror surfaces were once rumored to be secret doorways to unknown realms. Still waters, smooth crystals, broken glass and even ice each held the possibility of discovery.

One of them, the Mirror Matter Portal, is believed to be hidden in the Unicorn Kingdom. It's the last known magical gateway with the power to transform anyone who passes through it into their ocean self.

Kyrea has set off to find the lost portal and become something entirely new: a mermaid. Why? So she can join her best friend, Arlo the dragon, on a once-in-a-lifetime underwater adventure.

But the path to the portal is fraught with ancient magic, forgotten rules, and a twist that could turn their quest upside down, *literally*. With obstacles at every turn, challenges to overcome, and trials to endure, Kyrea begins to question whether this mission is even worth the trouble. Will she ever reach the portal, or are the unicorns themselves working to stop her?

UNDERWATER ADVENTURES 3

ETERNAL ENCHANTMENT 4

MAGICAL REALMS MERGE 5

UNVEILING ETERNITY 6

DOORWAY TO INFINITY 7

AS WELL AS SHORT STORIES
& SEPARATE SIDE ADVENTURES

About the Author

Kathleen J. Shields is an award-winning, multi-genre author best known for *The Hamilton Troll Adventures*, which earned First Place Best Educational Children's Series from the Texas Association of Authors. Her childhood creation *The First Unibear*, written at age ten, has won six awards and counting. She also received global recognition for *The First Unicorn* and her Christian fiction trilogy, *The Painting*.

While awaiting illustrations, Kathleen writes chapter books for tweens and general audiences, blending education with engaging stories to inspire a lifelong love of reading—and possibly writing. She openly shares her decades of knowledge with fellow writers, always eager to help others grow in their craft.

Kathleen also runs **Kathleen's Graphics**, offering web and graphic design services, custom book covers, interior formatting, book trailers, press releases, and more. She freelances for printing companies and publishers and thrives on learning new skills through creative challenges.

In addition, she writes an inspirational blog about her experiences as an author, entrepreneur, and Christian, offering thoughtful, uplifting insights meant to spark reflection and gather future readers.

For more information about the author and her books, please visit: www.KathleensBooks.com her blog at: www.KathleenJShields.com or follow her on numerous social media channels.

The Hamilton Troll Adventures

An award-winning educational series teaching young children social skills, animal characteristics, science and how to handle various real-life situations.

This multi-award-winning series consists of twelve fully illustrated, rhyming stories for bedtime up to 2nd grade. Included definitions to increase vocabulary along with a few fun games inside.

Also an award-winning Children's Cookbook, a Coloring book and a Curriculum Workbook to continue the education. Perfect for home school.

OTHER BOOKS BY THIS AUTHOR

The A to Z of Texas Wildflowers

Take a stroll through a spring field in Texas. Told in rhyme and perfect for children and lovers of nature.

Ghost Dogs

As a toddler Jamie develops an amazing gift, the ability to see Ghost Dogs. They look just like our past pets, just a bit more transparent.

Turtle Diaries

When a tortoise roams around a turtle sanctuary, fun, education and challenges ensue. He keeps a daily diary of his adventures.

Dream World Defenders

Ryan and his friends enter the dream world where they can do anything they can imagine. Except... Wake up.

ZITS From Outer Space

A Giant Scorpion, a Crab Attack and a Killer Wolf – What do these have in common? The zits on Jared's face! A boys will be boys with active imaginations kind of story.

Ally Cat, A Tale of Survival

Allison Catsworth gets knocked off of a cliff and instead of falling to her death, she transforms into a cat and lands on all four paws!

A Rainbow of Thanks

Kate walks into a rainbow and is transported to various places on the planet. She meets children of other cultures as she tries to get home.

A Rhyme for Everything

An extensive poetry collection of funny, inspirational, musical and simply creative rhyming verses for any occasion.

Kathleen J. Shields

The Painting

Gerald is given a blank canvas, so he paints a world, one that he loves so much – it comes to life!

The First Book of the Trilogy

The Painting 2

Benjamin, Gerald's son, finds a way to be born into the Painting so he can tell the inhabitants about his father, the Painter.

The Painting 3

Nevaeh, the granddaughter, she imagines herself into the painting. While she is only there in spirit, it is her desire to good that inspires others to act.

The Painting Trilogy Hard back

The full collection of stories in a collector's edition hardback book with beautiful dust jacket. A must have!

Dandy Lion, A Legend of Love & Loss

Dandy, the lion, loses a strand of hair each time he helps someone. He discovers he is sowing the seeds of love by doing good deeds.

The First Unibear

A bear rescues a horse that is actually a unicorn. Later, the bear gets a unicorn horn too. But why? A multi award winning inspirational rhyming story.

The First Unicorn

A young horse who helps others, gets bestowed a horn making him the first unicorn. What he can do is simply miraculous.

The First Unicorn (Bedtime Story)

A shorter version of the story making it perfect to read to young children at bedtime.

The Etiquette of Book Selling

A how to book encouraging authors to be their best and make a good first impression when out in the public.

How to Write, Market and Sell Children's Books

Everything a budding author should know before delving into the self-publishing arena.

The Dark Side of Self-Publishing

An authors tell-all about the many challenges, pitfalls, problems and scams that face a budding author, while showing all of the positives that come from following your dreams.

Pawsitive Vibes, Dogs

This fun devotional connects dog emotions and real stories to motivational messages that humans should to take to heart.

Have A Turtle-ific Day!

A creative daily devotional designed for turtle lovers of all different species, with fun ocean puns and soothing messages. Perfect to start your day with.

The Dog Who Cried Woof

Riley takes it upon himself to announce Daddy's return home, but turns it into a game that goes horribly wrong. *Short Story eBook*

Ethan's Reception

FiFi was not happy the day Ethan was brought home from the animal shelter, but Ethan was enthralled! *Short Story eBook*

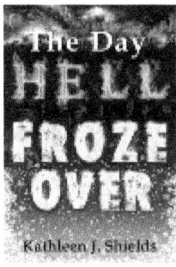

The Day Hell Froze Over

When the inhabitants of hell begin praying to God for some cold weather, the devil finds himself in quite the bind. *Short Story eBook*

The Kaitlyn Jones Trilogy

Kaitlyn discovers the gift of precognition, she's able to see things before they happen. She also discovers a telepathic bond with the guy who changed her life and the desire to help others with these gifts. Follow Kaitlyn through High School, her first job as a police officer. When she became a bodyguard, secret service and then secret agent!

Her Guarded Desire

Kristen must make a decision…

Her Bodyguard or Her Boyfriend

The flames of passion ignite when both men decide to work together to save her as well as themselves.

Erin Go Bragh Publishing publishes various genres of books for numerous authors. Their portfolio consists of a 1200-page Vietnamese to English Dictionary, Historical fiction, an award-winning children's educational series, multiple adult novels and memoirs, tween adventure stories, as well as Christian Fiction. Their objective is to promote literacy and education through reading and writing.

www.ErinGoBraghPublishing.com
Canyon Lake, Texas

℞EFERENCES

Green, Roger Lancelyn. *King Arthur and His Knights of the Round Table*. Illustrated by Lotte Reiniger, Puffin Books, 1953.

Burnett, Frances Hodgson. *The Secret Garden*. Frederick A. Stokes Company, 1911.

Grimm, Jacob, and Wilhelm Grimm. *Hansel and Gretel*. Translated by Margaret Hunt, 1884.

Johnson, Crockett. *Harold and the Purple Crayon*. Harper & Brothers, 1955.

White, E. B. *Charlotte's Web*. Illustrated by Garth Williams, Harper & Brothers, 1952.

"Jack and the Beanstalk." *English Fairy Tales*, edited by Joseph Jacobs, David Nutt, 1890.

Tobin, J. (2003). *To conquer the air: The Wright brothers and the great race for flight*. Free Press.

Verne, Jules. *20,000 Leagues Under the Sea*. Translated by William Butcher, Oxford University Press, 1991.

Carroll, Lewis. *Alice's Adventures in Wonderland*. Macmillan, 1865.

Andersen, H. C. (2004). *The complete fairy tales of Hans Christian Andersen* (L. S. Smith, Trans.). Dover Publications. (Original work published 1835)

O'Brien, R. (1971). *Mrs. Frisby and the rats of NIMH*. Atheneum.

Don Bluth. (Director). (1982). *The secret of NIMH* [Film]. Metro-Goldwyn-Mayer.

And numerous books that inspired a limitless imagination that soars beyond the stars! Every new story you read can be an inspiration. If you need new ideas, find a new book to read.

Thank you to my Beta Readers and editors.

To my very special friend, Angel, for being my sounding board, collaborator, and brainstormer while I curated these stories together. Also, for many of the interior illustrations.

A special thank you to Claire for your keen insight regarding the perspective of the dragon.